THE CAT'S OUT OF THE BAG

CYNTHIA TERELST

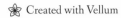

Thank you to my family and friends who constantly offer support and encouragement. But especially to Tegan, who is my constant sounding board and teacher. Without her, I would never have rediscovered my love of writing.

CHAPTER ONE

EVIE

I DON'T KNOW how I always got roped into training the new volunteers. Maybe they thought because I was friendly and laughed a lot, I would enjoy it. But I would rather have peace and quiet while I volunteered on Saturday morning at the cat shelter. Sometimes, I preferred the company of animals to that of humans. I didn't have to hide who I was with them. I never said no, though. Hopefully, this person would last longer than the average two weeks.

As Marjorie walked the new volunteer towards me, I considered him. He looked like he was in his mid-twenties, like me. The first thing I noticed was he could follow instructions. Even though it was hot outside, he managed to wear enclosed shoes. Usually, new volunteers turned up in thongs, which meant they couldn't do any work. They could only watch me instead.

Stopping, they turned towards a cage as Marjorie explained something to him, allowing me to study him closer. Extending from those work boots were well-tanned, muscular legs, which led up to a nice butt covered in khaki work shorts. I may have been happily single for two years and not on the hunt for a man, but that didn't mean I couldn't look and admire.

Seeing he was here on the weekend, it meant he wanted to be here. Some volunteers who attended during the week were only here to fulfil their community service requirements.

They continued towards me.

"Evie, this is Jesse. He is visiting from America and thought he would fill in some time volunteering."

Jesse held out his hand and smiled. I shook it firmly as he said, "Nice to meet you, Evie."

"Thanks. You, too," I replied, trying not to get lost in his blue eyes, which were accentuated by his grey t-shirt.

"I'll leave you in Evie's capable hands," Marjorie said before walking away.

"It's pretty straightforward. We follow the same routine every day," I said as I entered one of the cat enclosures.

I took him through the feeding and cleaning routine. He worked beside me and followed every instruction to the letter. It was like he had a photographic memory.

"How long have you been in Australia?"

"Three weeks."

"Just in Melbourne?" I asked as we started to fill the dry food bowls in the four enclosures at our end of the building.

"Yeah, it looked like a good place to start. It was voted the world's most liveable city for seven years in a row."

"Wow, I didn't know that."

"And, it has a low population density, which beats living in LA. Three thousand, eight hundred and fifty-eight people per square mile compared to 7,544."

"Sounds like you did your research."

He raised his head and looked at me before nodding.

"How long are you staying?"

"I haven't decided yet. Maybe a few months."

I tried to imagine being able to stay wherever I wanted for however long I wanted. It would never be possible. What sort of job would allow that?

He asked the next question so quickly I felt like he was trying to deflect the conversation away from himself.

"How long have you volunteered here for?"

"Nearly two years."

"You must enjoy it."

"I do. It's relaxing. The people are nice; we are like a little family. And I enjoy spending time with the cats."

He watched me while I spoke, nodding when I'd finished.

"See the old ginger cat over there? His name is Mike. He arrived a year after I started."

"He's been here a year?" Jesse asked, sounding surprised.

"Yes. We are a no-kill shelter. We keep them until they find a home."

"Why doesn't anyone want him?"

"He has a lot of things going against him, poor boy. His age, for starters. He is thirteen now. People are scared to adopt older animals. All they think about is sickness, cost, and death. But older animals give a lot of love. They are chill and less likely to destroy things, unlike kittens."

"How long do cats live for?"

"Usually, twelve to eighteen years."

"So, he has a good few years left?"

"Yeah. Unfortunately, he doesn't do himself any favours. When people come to meet the cats, he doesn't interact with them. He is partially deaf, so has trouble hearing them call his name. He sits and watches while other cats introduce themselves. By the time he is ready to say hello, the people have moved on. We try to tell them to be patient, but they are more interested in friendly cats."

"That's sad," Jesse said, looking at Mike.

"It is. But at least he is safe here. And we love him." I sent an affectionate smile Mike's way.

We continued working side-by-side in companionable silence. The cats lounged around, uninterested in our activity. It impressed me how Jesse never stood back to let me do the work. He helped with everything. I was also impressed with how his muscles flexed when he picked up the heavy bags of cat litter with ease.

When I brought the fresh meat out for the cats, they all jumped to attention. They weaved between our legs meowing, like their sudden desperation would make their food appear in their bowls quicker. One by one, as I put the food in their bowls, they sorted their hierarchy. Mike stood back and waited. I'm sure if cats could roll their eyes, he would have. He knew the food would come, and it didn't matter if he was first or last. He wasn't needy.

When we finished our enclosures, I gave Jesse a smile.

"Thanks for your help. It's easier with two of us. Are you ready for the fun part?"

"Fun part?"

"Yeah, where we interact with the cats. Do you want to join me?"

"Sure."

"There's some toys in that basket."

He moved towards the basket, looked inside, and then back at me. The way he ran his hand through his thick brown hair gave me the impression he didn't know what to do. It was an ordinary movement, but I couldn't help noticing the muscles in his upper arm as his sleeve lifted. What was wrong with me?

4

I turned my attention back to the basket. I didn't want him to feel uncomfortable, so I said, "Get out one of those sticks with a ribbon on it, and I'll show you what to do."

Smiling at me gratefully, he handed me the toy.

"Basically, you need to tease them with the ribbon—like this—to get them interested," I said as I dangled it in Sally's face. She was black and sleek. To me, she resembled a graceful lady the way she walked, with her head held high and her elongated body swaying. "When they become alert, their eyes will widen. Then, they will start to attack it."

Sally grabbed at the ribbon. I pulled it out of her reach, encouraging her to climb the post and chase it. I laughed as she defied gravity, bouncing off the walls to chase the ribbon. When I looked back at Jesse, he was standing next to Mike, patting him, smiling.

"Does Mike like to play?"

"Sometimes. Why don't you give it a try?"

I watched the pair of them as they played. Mike eagerly reached for the ribbon. When he caught it, he wrestled with it, rolling and biting and clawing. It surprised me how much Mike was interacting with Jesse. Usually, he lost interest after a few minutes. But he played and purred and smooched for at least ten. Jesse was so focused on him, I may as well have not been in the enclosure with them.

After we had given each of the cats some playtime, I said, "You can go now. That's it for the day."

He started walking to the door. When I didn't follow, he turned to me.

"Are you coming?"

"No, I'm staying for a while. I usually end my visit reading to the cats."

His sky-blue eyes widened. "Read to the cats?"

"Bloody oath," I said, trying to hold in my grin as he

stared at me, scratching his head. I knew what I had just said would confuse him. "It's an Australian saying. It means, yes, I'm serious."

I laughed at him, and his eyes crinkled as he laughed in return.

"You guys sure have some weird sayings."

"You haven't heard anything yet," I said, still laughing. "The cats enjoy listening to people read. The rhythmic sound relaxes them. They come and sit with me or on me. It helps them socialise in a non-pressured environment."

"What do you read?"

I wondered if he was making fun of me, but his face was serious.

"Harry Potter. But they will listen to anything. We've introduced the reading program to the local school. The kids love it. Some don't have pets at home or have never met a cat. You should see their faces when they're first introduced; it's like magic. And the teachers have said how much their reading skills have improved. It's a win-win."

"That's excellent. Literacy is important; we need to read and write every day. Thirty-two million adults in America are illiterate." He paused, looking like he wanted to say more. "I'll see you next week," he said instead, turning to leave.

I watched him walk away. His butt filled his shorts nicely. At least there would be something good to look at if he decided to return next week.

CHAPTER TWO

JESSE

I DIDN'T THINK I'd enjoy my morning of volunteering as much as I did. Evie was a joy to be around. She chatted, smiled, and laughed the whole morning. Her instructions were as clear as her sparkling blue eyes.

When she suggested I play with the cats, I had no idea what to do. I didn't have pets growing up. It was another expense we couldn't afford. And when I got a place of my own, I didn't even think about buying a pet. Money wasn't a problem, but I guess I didn't understand the companionship a pet could bring.

My grandma, who was my biggest supporter, always loved cats. The cats she had were lap cats; they were not active and didn't play. My grandma was the reason why I decided to volunteer at the cat rescue in the first place. It was to honor her memory and to help me feel close to her.

Evie saw my hesitation when she pointed to the cat toys and was kind in her response. She didn't look at me like I was stupid. Instead, she showed me what to do without pause. Kindness was a quality to be admired.

As I walked into the office to sign out, Marjorie looked up at me and said, "Did you have a good morning, Jesse?"

"Yes, Evie's a great teacher," I replied.

"Thank you for your help. Will we see you again next week?"

"Yes. I'd love to come back. Thank you."

"Next Saturday is the first Saturday of the month, so we'll all be going out for lunch. I hope you can join us."

"That would be great. See you next week."

When Saturday came again, I was eager to spend time with the cats. I met Evie inside the enclosure. I greeted each cat by name, giving them a quick pat in their favorite spots before getting to work.

Tilting her head, Evie watched me. Her blue eyes, vibrant against her olive skin, regarded me as I started cleaning the litter trays exactly as she had taught me.

"You have a good memory," she said as she started working beside me, tossing her brown ponytail over her shoulder. She was perceptive. No one had picked up on my memory that quickly before.

"It's one of my many talents," I replied casually. I didn't want to elaborate.

"Did you hear that a literacy foundation gave the cat shelter one hundred thousand dollars to build a reading nook?" She asked, her voice animated.

"Yeah, Marjorie told me when I came in."

I didn't need Marjorie to tell me, though, seeing it was my foundation who donated.

"It's great. More kids will be able to join the program. And they will be able to read in comfort, with nice soft couches or bean bags, and a climate-controlled environment. My gosh, imagine how much extra contact the cats will have."

"Everyone's a winner."

Her eyes were wide, and her smile beamed with excitement. I couldn't help smiling in return.

"What did you do this week? Did you check out some sights?" Evie asked in her cheerful tone.

"I went to the National Gallery. It was fascinating. Did you know they have over 75,000 pieces of art, and you can download copies of over half of them for free?"

"I didn't know that. It sure would be a good way to decorate your walls. Did you see any Hans Heysen paintings? I love his use of soft light."

"Yes, and they had some paintings from Nora, his daughter, too. It was a special exhibition."

"What was her art like?"

"Impressive. Her use of color was stronger than her father's. She was the first woman to win the Archibald Prize, and the first Australian woman to be appointed as an official war artist. Her assignment was to show the women's war effort."

Evie's eyes were wide. "I didn't even know she existed."

"You wouldn't believe what one of the headlines was when she won the Archibald."

Evie stopped working and turned towards me.

"What?"

"Girl Painter Who Won an Art Prize is also a Good Cook."

Evie's jaw clenched. "You're shitting me?"

"Nope. They couldn't help but make an irrelevant comment about her gender rather than her artistic skills."

Evie's face was still hard. "And still, to this day, it feels like perceptions and beliefs have not changed much."

"They should teach these things in school. Even back then, she was a revolutionary in saying things like 'there was

9

no reason whatsoever why women should not be as good as painters as men.'"

"A woman after my own heart," Evie declared. "There is no reason women can't do *anything* as good as men."

She bent back down, sneaking a sideways glance at me as we changed task. I felt like she was checking if I was still following her instructions from last week, but she didn't comment.

"What did you do this week?" I asked her.

"Worked, mostly. I have a dog walking business."

That explained her toned legs and tan.

"That's cool. How does that work?"

"I have an app I use for client bookings and to create schedules for the walkers. I've tried to optimize over time; travelling time used to have a big effect on how many dogs we could walk. Most of our work is in apartment buildings now. I can usually get a full day's work out of one or two buildings. It reduces travel time and increases profit."

I nodded. It was a smart way to run a business. A lot of time poor, white-collar workers would opt-in. The statistics on pets living in apartments was interesting. I learnt about them when deciding where to stay during my Australian visit. I wasn't looking at pets in particular, but wanted to know about the density of living in the major cities, which then drew the facts and figures out for pets. I knew there were over 279,000 apartments in Victoria. At ninety-four percent, 262,000 of those were in the city. On average, thirty-eight percent of households own dogs. The percentage would likely be lower for apartments. Working with a conservative estimate of ten percent, you would be looking at 26,000 dogs. That's a lot of dogs needing walks.

My mind worked fast. The pause in conversation was short.

"That's smart business. There must be at least 26,000 dogs in the dog walking pool in Melbourne alone. You must be busy."

She regarded me again with those thoughtful eyes.

"I'm turning away clients all the time. I could expand, but I don't like to complicate things."

Like many Australians I'd met so far, she was easy-going and averse to adding stress to her life. I liked their way of thinking. Part of the reason I was in Australia was to re-evaluate where I was going in life. My grandma often reminded me I needed to do what made me happy. I could afford to do that now. I just needed to figure out what it was that made me happy. I didn't have a chance to explore different interests growing up. My parents only had one interest for me to follow. Money.

When we finished cleaning, Evie gave me one of her big smiles. "We have fifteen minutes before we head off for lunch. How about you stay in here and play with the cats while I put this stuff away?"

"Are you sure? I'm happy to help you."

"Nah, she'll be right."

Another one of those quirky Australian sayings? Was the *she*, she was referring to, herself?

As she disappeared, I got a toy and encouraged some running and jumping. To add to the fun, I added some commentary like we were playing a Quidditch match. I joined the running and jumping. Feeling light-hearted, I laughed. I didn't realize Evie had returned until I saw her standing at the door, smiling at me.

"Harry Potter fan, are you?"

"Who isn't?" I said, shrugging.

"Only people with no brains. Are you ready?"

"Sure am."

I WALKED with Evie and the other volunteers to the local pub. I learned early on that a pub is like an American bar, except they're family-friendly, and it's not just about watching sports on TV. The pub scene is part of Australian culture. A few times, when I'd met people while out surfing, they'd invite me to the pub afterward. We'd have a meal or some beers and chat.

I watched Evie as we walked along. She had so much energy it was like every step incorporated a bounce. She talked to everyone, from the older ladies and their husbands to the younger volunteers. At one point, she turned around, her long brown hair flowing with the movement, and looked back. When her eyes fell on me, she smiled and then resumed her conversation. My skin warmed at her gaze.

"Evie's nice, isn't she?" Marjorie asked from beside me, her brown eyes watching me.

I blushed when I realized she had been watching me watching Evie.

"She is. She's friendly and laughs a lot. She is not afraid to say what she thinks about women's rights," I said, remembering her reaction to the news headline.

Clarissa, an older lady with a blue tint in her hair, said, "When she started with us two years ago, she was very sad and troubled. She'd a bad breakup and was struggling."

"Clarissa," Marjorie chided, "Don't speak out of turn."

Ignoring Marjorie, Clarissa continued, "She sure has turned things around. She has her own business and loves the animals she works with. The repeat business she gets is a testament to her dedication." Lowering her voice, she added, "She is so independent and happy knowing her life is complete without a man, but it would be nice to see her with one."

"Clarissa, enough. Jesse doesn't want to hear your gossip."

I looked at Evie, thinking Jesse was indeed happy to listen to Clarissa's gossip. But I knew it was wrong and was ashamed at the thought. It should be Evie's choice to share that information with me. But I was curious to know what could have caused her to be so broken. And how she rebuilt herself.

Strength. Resilience. Kindness. Happiness. Everything everyone should strive for. Everything Evie had.

When we got to the pub, Clarissa took over the seating arrangements, making sure Evie and I were seated together. I grinned to myself as I saw Marjorie rolling her eyes at her.

The pub had a homely atmosphere. Wooden furniture made it feel warm and welcoming. Luscious plants hung from the ceiling, giving the feeling of being in a living space. Light filtered in from skylights, adding to the warm ambience.

"It's nice here," I said to Evie.

"As flash as a rat with a gold tooth."

When I looked at her blankly, she laughed. I was sure she got pleasure out of confusing me with Australian sayings.

"It was a bit of a dump before, a rat, but they have put a lot of effort into impressing us and changing our perception, the gold tooth."

Evie and I shared the menu. She flicked the pages back and forth. My fingers grazed hers as we both reached to turn a page, and a quick spark lit my fingertips.

"I can't decide. What are you getting?" she asked.

"I thought I'd give the kangaroo with quandong a try."

"That sounds good. Let's go up and order. I'll decide when we get there," she said, getting up and handing the menu over to Marjorie.

As we stood in line, she bounced on her toes. It was like she could hardly contain her energy; she had to keep moving. Maybe she was nervous. Last week, when I watched her reading to the cats, she stayed quite still.

"Have you decided yet?"

"No. I love beef. What sort of steaks were there again?"

I recited the menu.

"How much is the three-hundred-gram rump?"

"Twenty-five dollars."

When she smiled astutely at me, I realized she was testing me. Perceptive, and cunning. I tensed. I didn't like people knowing about my exceptional memory. Once they knew, they treated me differently. They either wanted to exploit me or make me do party tricks. And when they found out about my money, they were worse. I wanted people to like me for me. Being here was that chance.

"That was sneaky," I said, as she studied me closely.

"Just testing a hunch," she said, giving me a knowing smile. "Don't worry. Your secret is safe with me."

I hoped so.

CHAPTER THREE

EVIE

WHEN OUR FOOD ARRIVED, Jesse stared at my three-hundred-gram steak. Looking at me with wide eyes, he said, "That's huge. Are you going to eat all that?"

"Easy. You don't get a body like this on salad alone. I'm going to get another drink. Do you want one?"

"I'll come with you," he said, getting up after me.

Once we were out of earshot, he said to me, "There is nothing wrong with your body."

The comment surprised me. I wasn't fishing for a compliment.

"Jesse, were you checking out my arse?" I asked as he fell into step beside me.

The red rising in his cheeks gave me the answer.

"I was just kidding. It's not like you can miss it anyway," I said, laughing.

He looked at me seriously, before saying, "You should stop being self-deprecating. There's nothing wrong with curves." Then he looked away quickly, perhaps embarrassed by his declaration.

I didn't have a chance to answer before the bartender

asked for our order. Even if I'd had a chance to reply, I don't know what I would have said. I don't know if he was being nice or if he was trying to crack onto me. I didn't feel comfortable with the second option. I liked my uncomplicated life. A man would complicate it. And after Nick, I found it hard to trust men.

During our meal, Jesse asked, "Are there any footpaths close to the city where we can hike?"

"There are footpaths everywhere. What do you mean?" Georgia asked him, raising her perfectly shaped eyebrows. I sipped on my beer, hiding my smile. At the ripe old age of twenty-five, Georgia was still so youthful, in words and actions. Her strong expressions always amused me. Usually, they didn't stop at her face, either. Her long limbs would often add to her countenance, as they moved emphatically.

"Paths where you can walk in the wilderness," Jesse said. "What do you call it here?"

"Bushwalks," Georgia said, laughing. "We walk in the bush on a track."

"Footpaths in Australia are like your sidewalks in the states," I said to him.

"That makes no sense," he said, shaking his head. "Are there any bushwalks close to the city?"

"There's a walk at Werribee Gorge. Evie, remember we were going to go last year, but it rained?" Georgia said, looking at me.

"Yeah, that's pretty close to the city. Less than an hour."

"We should go," Georgia said. She pulled her long blonde hair back in a ponytail like she was preparing to leave right at that moment, her eyes wide with excitement. "I've got nothing on tomorrow. Who wants to come?"

"How tough is this walk?" Jonas asked. "If it's not as

hard as the walk you two took us on last year, where we nearly died, Miranda and I are in. Aren't we, sis?"

Jonas looked over at his twin, who nodded in response. It was remarkable how their eyes were identical; upturned and a rich brown, with long lashes any girl would die for.

"It's meant to be tough, but I'm sure we'll manage," I said.

"I'd like to join you all," Jesse said.

"Great," Georgia said. "If it's just us five, we can carpool."

Her excitement was infectious. We spent the remainder of lunch making preparations.

As we were finishing up, I leant over and asked," What did you think of the kangaroo?'

"It has a strong, gamey flavour."

"The quandong would have helped cut through the strong flavour."

"It did. It was sweet and tangy, the perfect accompaniment."

WE GOT out of the car and looked around. The ground was brown dirt, and there was little ground cover, even where it extended into the bush. Because the area had been cleared to create the carpark, the surrounding bush wasn't dense. The nearby gum trees were juvenile, only a couple of metres tall, their trunks no thicker than a leg. Due to their young age, their green leaves were vibrant and glossy. The track was obvious and cut a clear path through the trees.

"Drop bears are known to inhabit this area, so try not to get separated," I said, giving the others a sly wink.

"Drop bears?" Jesse asked, his voice dropping an octave.

"They sort of look like koalas and live up in trees," Jonas said.

Jesse looked around, peering into the trees.

"They call them drop bears because they drop out of the trees, from as high as eight metres," I said in a serious tone.

"Their fangs are huge," Georgia said, baring her teeth and hunching her shoulders, adding to the drama. The act looked so out of place on her tall, slim body, I tried not to laugh.

Miranda turned away, covering her mouth to stifle a giggle.

"They drop onto their prey, including us humans, stunning us, and then they attack our face," I said.

"They don't just attack your face, they bite it off," Jonas added.

Georgia shuddered, feigning fear.

Jesse stood there looking between us. A smile started to emerge but disappeared when we all stared back at him, our faces stern, no hint of humour in our eyes.

"You're joking, right?"

"We're dead serious. Don't get separated. They won't attack us if we're together." I lifted my backpack onto my shoulders. "They say vegemite behind the ears repels them, but I think that's a myth," I said, hoping it would add a ring of truth.

Jesse continued looking up into the treetops, as he put his backpack on. I turned away from him, smiling. There were no drop bears at Werribee Gorge.

"Don't bother looking for them. The first time you'll see one is when it's latched to your face," Jonas said as he fell into step behind us.

We followed the wide dirt track, Georgia and I taking

the lead. It was easy going. The bush encroached on us from both sides. If we walked too close to the edge of the track, strands of tall grass brushed against our legs. Some trees stood tall, their leaves green and vibrant, rustling in the slight breeze. Their strong trunks showing nature's true beauty; dark red bark peeled away in strips, revealing smooth cream trunks. Smaller trees had straggly limbs pointing in all directions, like abstract pieces of art.

Nothing beat the fresh, pure eucalyptus smell of the bush. It was invigorating. People tried to bottle the smell in detergents and the like, but it could never match the natural smell in the bush. It wasn't overpowering; it was subtle, like a delicate layer. I breathed in deep, letting it cleanse my lungs.

Arriving at Falcons Lookout, we stood on the grey rock cliff top and took in the view. The gorge stretched out as far as the eye could see, deep and undulating, covered in patches of trees along its rocky ascent. The river wound its way through it, its path dissecting east from west, a deep ravine. It was stunning.

As Jesse stood beside me, he drew in his breath. His wide eyes examined the scene in front of us before he turned to me, smiling. My mouth and heart smiled in response. I rarely saw males openly appreciate nature. He was different; he never tried to hide his feelings. Like yesterday, when he bluntly told me there was nothing wrong with curves.

"It's beautiful," he said.

I nodded in agreement.

"We're heading down there," I said, pointing to the river. From where we stood, it looked like a long and difficult descent. "And then up the other side."

The track narrowed, hugging the ridge all the way down

to the river, so we walked single file along the rocky ground. The only sound that broke the silence was the rhythm of our steady footsteps. Every now and then, the song of a magpie would cut through the still air. It had a beautiful, lyrical song; fluty and warbling.

"Did you hear that bird?" I asked Jesse, who was behind me.

"Yes."

"That's a magpie. You know you're in the bush when you hear their glorious song. They can be dangerous, though. They like to swoop people, especially during breeding season. They fly down low, trying to attack your head, to gouge your eyes out. Even if they don't connect, you feel the air move as they swoosh past. It's terrifying. They keep coming back to get you until you get out of their territory."

"Jeez, is there anything in Australia that doesn't try to kill you?"

"Not much," I said, laughing.

"You have twelve deadly snakes, including the most venomous in the world."

"Don't forget about our deadly spider, too," Miranda said.

"What spider?" Jesse asked. There was a slight pause in his step.

"The funnel web. It's a pretty sneaky bastard," I replied.

"What do you mean?" Jesse's voice had risen slightly.

"It likes to hide in shoes and clothing left on the floor to avoid drying out," I told him.

"Not only that, if it's in the water, it can trap itself in a bubble of water to breathe and float," Jonas said. "So, even if you think it may be dead, it's probably not!"

"You're not serious."

"Unfortunately, he is. That has got to be the worst trick a spider can play on humanity. I hate spiders," I said, shuddering at the thought. Funnel webs were really ugly mothers, and the way they reared up, ready to strike, was terrifying.

"We have anti-venom," Georgia said.

"That's not much help when some things can kill you in minutes," Jesse said, shaking his head as I turned to look at him.

"Don't worry, they live in Sydney," I said, trying to reassure him.

"Hey, what about all the deadly things in the water?" Georgia said, her light voice indicating her enjoyment.

"Like what?" Jesse asked as I looked at him. I could see his Adam's apple bobbing.

"There's jellyfish. One so small you'd be lucky to see it, and another one that has tentacles two metres long," Jonas said.

"Great," Jesse's tone was deadpan.

"We have crocodiles and sharks, too," Miranda said.

"Crocodiles are up north. You don't have to worry about them here," I said.

"Because that makes it so much better."

I shrugged.

"There's more," Georgia said. She was enjoying this way too much.

"I don't think I need to hear any more, thanks."

"Not that many people die from animal attacks," I said.

"Yeah, right, because that's reassuring."

As we emerged from the shade of the trees, the heat of the day greeted us. It was early summer; the day was cool compared to what it could be. If it had been a forty-two-degree day, there was no way we would attempt this walk.

"Wow, you can really feel the difference when you step out from the shade," Jesse said.

"What's the weather like where you're from?" I asked.

"Los Angeles is like here, wet in winter, dry in summer. It doesn't get too hot there."

"It can get really hot here. On a forty-two-degree day, when you open your front door, it's like the heat from a furnace hitting your face."

"Forty-two is like 107 for us. What about winter?"

"Miserable and freezing."

"Well defined seasons by the sounds of it."

"Yep."

When we reached the river, we looked back up to the lookout. The gorge towered spectacularly above us.

Along the tranquil river, the rocky bank was interspersed with sandy beaches. Vegetation made it all the way to the water's edge in some places. Reeds barely moved in the still water.

I walked along the bank until I found a flat rock. Sitting, I took my backpack off and reached in to grab a snack. As I bit into a protein bar, I considered the climb on the other side. It looked like our legs would get a decent workout.

Georgia sat with Jesse and Jonas a few metres away, talking. My name caught my attention, but I couldn't hear what they were saying.

"Where are we crossing the river?" Miranda asked, drawing my attention away.

I got up and stood next to her, surveying the rocks.

"Here, I think," I said, walking to a line of rocks that looked easy to navigate. They were evenly spread, and we wouldn't need to stretch our legs too far between rocks, risking our balance.

"Are you guys ready?" Miranda asked.

"Yes," Jesse said, rising. He looked at me and smiled.

My heart quickened a beat.

Miranda took the lead, crossing the river first. The climb on the other side was steep and long, requiring some rock-scrambling.

Half way up, we stopped for a rest and drink. I sucked in a breath as I examined the view. There was a mixture of undulating hills and craggy cliffs making their way down to the river, their sharpness changing to a delicate softness as they met the horizon. Shadow and light played off the dips and curves of the hills, reminding me of paintings of naked ladies by French artists from years gone by, voluptuous and sensual. The cliff faces varied in colour from a steely grey to a rich rust. The shadows defined their sharp edges and ruggedness. The river cut its path between them, contained by the ancient layers of sedimentary rock, before widening out again.

I pressed my t-shirt against my back to soak up the sweat before we headed off again.

Hearing a screech above us, I looked up to the gloriously clear, powder-blue sky. A wedge-tailed eagle soared above us; its wings spread wide as it glided effortlessly. I couldn't believe my eyes and stopped so I could watch it make its way across the sky.

"Look at that," I said in wonder.

"Wow, is that a wedgie?" Georgia asked.

"Yes, the tail gives it away. And look at the wingspan, it must be at least two metres."

We all stared up at the sky. Even Miranda in the lead had stopped.

"Farmers once thought wedge-tailed eagles were a menace. They shot thousands of them because they thought they killed their livestock. But we know now their preferred diets are rabbits or lamb carcasses," I said for Jesse's benefit.

"Such a waste," he said. He was standing so close I felt his body heat. Instinctively, I moved away, trying not to make it obvious by walking to Miranda.

The trail went to the top and then back down to the river. Our track was no longer a track, but a ledge along the cliff face. The rocky cliffs dropped down to the river below us. Holding onto the cable attached to the cliff face, I kept checking ahead and then back down to my feet continuously. One slip would find me falling over the edge. At a narrow part, I manoeuvred my body, so I was facing the cliff and shimmied sideways. Pausing, I leant backwards, away from the cliff, peering at the river below us. The river, which was as calm as ever, did not replicate my increased heart rate. Jesse, who was beside me, didn't mirror my move. He kept himself close to the cliff face and stared at it.

We made it back to our river crossing and up to the lookout. Jesse sat behind me, away from the edge of the cliff, while I sat with my legs dangling over.

"That was fun. It was harder than I expected," Jesse said.

"Yeah, I don't think you'll be going surfing tomorrow. Your legs will be sore," Jonas said, laughing.

Well, that explained the deep tan and muscles.

We stood up to leave. When Jesse lifted his shirt to wipe his face, there was a lot of flesh showing. He didn't have a six-pack, but his stomach was certainly flat and sculpted. I found it hard to draw my eyes away. The wiping movement caused his shorts to shift a little, showing his tan line just below his waist band. Realising my eyes were lingering too long, a blush rose on my face.

"I reckon we should go to the pub for a couple of drinks before we head home," Georgia said.

"Yeah, nothing wrong with a bit of self-medication," Miranda added.

I smiled to myself. Those two never passed up an opportunity for a drink.

Georgia walked beside me on the way back to the car. She slowed her pace, so the distance increased between the front group and us.

"Jesse's nice," she said.

Narrowing my eyes, I looked at her.

"Yes, he is."

"Maybe you two should go out or something," she said, glancing at me.

"You know I'm not interested in having a relationship."

"Come on, Evie, not every guy is like Nick."

"Nick wasn't like Nick...until he was."

"I'm sure Nick was always a narcissist. He just hid it well in the beginning."

That was true. If I looked back now, I could see the signs. But I was young then, sixteen, and he was twenty. He did a good job grooming me. He told me his story, drawing me in, with tales of his constantly disappointed parents—parents so like my own—I thought I had found a kindred spirit, someone who understood me. But it was all lies to lure me in. He gave me attention, making me feel special. His charm and flattery were second to none. That was the beginning. It soon changed.

Soon, he criticised me without a second thought. But if I had something negative to say about him, he would lose his shit. He needed constant praise and admiration, but it was a one-way street. He was manipulative beyond description. He made me feel bad for wanting to spend time with others.

So much so, all my friends disappeared from my neglect. I was isolated. He would read my mail and listen to phone calls.

I closed my eyes and took a deep breath as I remembered those last few months when the abuse stepped up tenfold and climaxed the day I left. I couldn't risk putting myself in that situation again. Being on my own was better. Safer.

"He's probably leaving soon anyway. So, there's no point." I tried to erase the idea from her mind.

"He told Jonas and me he had no plans to leave yet," she said as we reached the car.

I rolled my eyes. My attempt at redirection hadn't worked very well.

"Just think about it."

I didn't need to.

CHAPTER FOUR

JESSE

I WALKED UP to the bar with Evie by my side, ready to order a round of beers for our group. She stood beside me, and in her usual fashion, didn't stay still. She stretched up on her toes, holding herself there for a couple of seconds before sinking back down. Then she shifted her weight from foot to foot, almost like a tennis player waiting for a serve.

I glanced at her. She responded with her easy-going smile, before saying, "Just working my calves. Don't want them to tighten up."

When the bartender arrived, I ordered our beers.

"You American?" he asked, scratching the grey stubble on his chin.

"Yes."

"You lot been out to the gorge?"

"Yeah. We did the circuit walk. It was stunning, so beautiful and peaceful."

"See any drop bears?" he asked, giving me a toothy grin.

"No. Thank goodness. Evie said if we stuck together, they wouldn't bother us."

"Evie, huh? Like the song?" he asked, turning his gaze on her.

"Yes, like the song," she said, returning his smile.

To my surprise, he started singing as he poured our beers. "Evie, Evie, Evie, let your hair hang down..."

"You were named after a song?"

"Not just any song. An eleven-minute song considered to be one of the most perfect songs in the world."

That's fitting, I thought to myself while giving her a smile.

Arriving back at the table, we heard the other three talking excitedly. Evie sat next to Georgia on the bench, and I squeezed in beside her. Her leg started bouncing next to mine. I thought it must have been nervous tension. No one could harbor so much extra energy. I rested my hand on her leg, trying to reassure her there was nothing to be nervous about. I was expecting her to relax. Instead, she became as stiff as a post. I felt stupid, I shouldn't have touched her like that when we hardly knew each other.

"Sorry," I whispered as I moved my hand away.

She bit her lip before giving me a small smile.

"There's a twenty-twenty match on tomorrow," Jonas said. "We should go, show Jesse some culture."

"Twenty-twenty?" I asked.

"It's a short version of a cricket match. Each team bowls twenty overs," Evie explained in her patient way.

"I'd love to go," I told them all.

Miranda gave an excited clap.

"I don't know if I can leave work early enough. I have a full day of clients tomorrow," Evie said.

My heart dropped. I tapped my fingers on the table, trying to think of how to solve the problem. It wouldn't be the same without her there.

"How about I come and help you? I've got nothing planned for the day."

"That's a perfect solution. Evie, please say you'll come," Georgia said.

Evie was quiet for a moment while we all watched her. I'm sure we all held our collective breath waiting for her to answer.

"OK," she said, shrugging.

EVIE PICKED me up in the morning. Her hatchback was clean, almost like it had just come off the showroom floor. As I got into the car, I was humming the tune to *Evie*. I couldn't get it out of my head after listening to it on Spotify the night before. She rolled her eyes at me.

"Sorry, it's so darn catchy. I can't get it out of my head."

"Here, get something else in your head," she said, turning the radio on. A Pink song came on and we sang together. It surprised me how I didn't feel self-conscious with her, like singing along with someone was something I did every day. She made me feel comfortable, and I liked that.

"Jesse, look," Evie said, pointing to the sky.

A group of colorful balloons floated on the horizon.

"I'd love to do that one day. It looks so peaceful," she said wistfully, looking at the balloons. Then turning to me, she said, "We don't have time today to run through the induction or any training. We'll just need to walk the dogs together; taking one each will save time."

"OK. That's a good idea. I wouldn't want to get lost."

"With a memory like yours, I am sure you would have no problem memorizing a map." She said it casually, like it was no big deal. I tried not to tense at the mention of my abilities.

"True, but I don't know where we're going, so I don't have a map to study."

She nodded.

"There's a polo shirt in the bag for you."

I pulled the teal shirt out of the bag and read the business name, 'Hit the Frog and Toad.' I was bewildered. It was obviously another weird Australian saying.

"It means hit the road," Evie explained.

"That's a smart name. I love the color of the shirts too. You've got good taste."

She glanced at me and gave me a smile before saying, "Thanks."

We talked while the traffic inched its way towards the city. My phone rang in my pocket. Pulling it out, I looked at the number. It was my mother. Cringing, I hit the ignore button so it would go to voicemail. I had successfully avoided speaking to her for nearly five weeks and wanted to keep it that way.

Evie glanced at me before turning her attention back to the road.

"It was my mother," I said, staring out the windshield.

"You can call her back if you want. I won't think you're rude if you talk to her in front of me."

"I'd rather not." I continued staring out the window.

"OK." Evie's response was quick.

Hell, my mother wasn't even here, and she managed to get in the way. I didn't want Evie to think she was the problem.

"I don't get along particularly well with my mother. If I can avoid speaking to her, I do."

Evie and I stared out of the windshield, lost in our own thoughts.

My mother had a way of ruining relationships for me.

When I was a young teenager, she entered me into contest after contest—spelling bees, memory championships, math competitions. We travelled far and wide to reap in the rewards she so badly wanted. We met the same people at many of these events, and I became close to a girl named Susie-May.

We would sit together backstage, joking and laughing. Usually, we sat in a corner away from everyone else so as to not disturb them. We would practice together, making waiting time fun. Susie-May did the competitions for fun. She was not forced into it and could stop at any time. My different circumstances gleaned genuine sympathy from her. I looked forward to seeing her. My world was virtually limited to school, studying, and competitions. Susie-May was the only person my age who I spent time with.

One afternoon, as we were waiting for the final, my mother stormed backstage. She grabbed Susie-May by the arm and hauled her out of the chair, dragging her into the corridor while I scurried after them. Mom's eyes were wide, showing the whites. Wild. I grabbed at her arm, trying to make her stop. She flung her hand back, smacking me across the face. My eyes watered.

Susie-May was pushed against the wall, my mother pinning her there, her full adult weight against Susie-May's shoulder.

"Mom! Stop!"

"Stay out of this, Jesse," she snarled. Spittle built up in the corners of her mouth.

I tried again to pull her away. My gangly body no match

against a full-grown woman in rage. Susie-May stared at her, her features swinging between defiance and terror.

"You stay away from my son."

She pushed harder on Susie-May's shoulder. Then she had both hands on her, holding her there, sneering in her face.

I couldn't breathe. Why wasn't anyone coming to help us?

"I know you are trying to sabotage this competition. I know you are trying to turn him against me."

Susie-May looked back at her, every inch of her body shaking. Her frightened eyes looked at me, begging me for help.

I squeezed into the space between them, pushing my body against Susie-May's, breaking my mother's grip. She took hold of me instead, her nostrils flaring, and I flinched at her touch.

"Mom, stop it. Susie-May didn't do anything wrong. She's my friend."

"You may be a smart boy, but you are one of the stupidest people I know. In what world do you think anyone would actually like you? Or want to be your friend?"

She stared at me, daring me to argue with her. Her grip tightened. I knew the only way to placate her was to agree. So, I did.

She dragged me away, back to the waiting area. I looked back at Susie-May. She was hugging herself, crying.

As we competed in the final, Susie-May wouldn't look at me. She knew the answers to questions but got them wrong deliberately. It was her last chance to show me she was my friend. She knew what my fate would be if I had gone home, having not beaten her.

I never saw Susie-May again.

After that, I'd resisted forming friendships.

Evie broke into my memory, "I think a lot of people have relationships like that with their parents. You're not alone."

Evie's words put me at ease. I relaxed as we stopped at the traffic lights. Glancing at Evie, I was relieved to see an understanding smile.

WE ARRIVED at a multi-story apartment building. Keying a code into the security pad, Evie explained the building manager reserved a parking spot for her. It meant she didn't take up a visitor's spot all day.

We walked the dogs in pairs throughout the day, matching their walking styles. Some liked a good old power walk, giving our legs and hearts a good workout. Others liked to meander around the block, investigating things that took their interest. Evie said it was all about keeping the dogs happy. She could tell you the life story of every dog we walked. She could tell you their good habits and bad habits.

"We'll walk Benny and Bones next. Benny is old. He likes to take things slow. Bones doesn't care either way. He gets distracted by every little thing."

We didn't walk far but still spent the same amount of time with the dogs. Bones stopped at just about every tree and pole, cocking his leg. Evie and Benny would keep walking, knowing we would catch up.

"You better not stand downwind when he does that. I learnt the hard way how far pee can travel on a breeze."

She laughed joyfully at the dogs' little quirks as if everything they did warmed her heart. I knew she was warming mine.

Bones made another pit stop. Evie continued on slowly before stopping to chat with a middle-aged couple. Benny sat at her feet, staring up at her with complete adoration. He nudged her with his nose. Bending down, she picked him up, caressing his ears as she spoke. It had only taken one nudge from him, that's how attentive she was. She set off again and I continued to watch her as Bones and I caught up. She said a friendly hello to everyone we passed, compelling me to do the same.

"THANKS FOR YOUR HELP TODAY," Evie said as she pulled up in front of the house.

"You're welcome."

I liked the way she always made a point to thank me, whether it was at the shelter, if I bought her a drink, if I said something nice to her, and even just now. Most other people took me for granted. I could buy a house for my mother and not even get a thank you. Evie didn't need to give me a thank you today. I should be thanking her for sharing her time with me. It was a privilege.

"How about we meet at the train station later and catch a train into the city? It's an easy walk to the Melbourne Cricket Ground, MCG, for short, from Flinders Street Station."

"Sure."

I felt a lightness at the thought of spending more time with Evie. Her happiness and energy were infectious. The only time she seemed uncomfortable with me was when I touched her leg yesterday. Clarissa said her last relationship was bad. Georgia and Jonas reiterated that yesterday when we were sitting by the river. They didn't go into detail, but the way she tensed up when I touched her made me wonder.

WHEN WE ARRIVED at the traffic lights outside Flinders Street Station, Evie told me to turn around. From the inside, you would never have known the station was so grand. The red brick building, rendered a rich yellow, covered two street fronts. On the corner, wide steps led to an archway under which there was a row of nine clocks, showing the train departure times for each of the train lines. Right at the top of the station was a green copper dome.

"When we're going to meet people, we will say 'meet you under the clocks.' Everyone in Melbourne knows it's these clocks we mean. Before the clocks were automatic, a man would change the departure times by hand, nine hundred times in eight hours." She pointed in the direction of the clock tower at the other end of the station and said, "There's a ballroom up there on the third floor. It was very popular in the fifties and sixties. Last I heard, it was in ruin. I wish they would restore it. Imagine taking dance classes up there; it would feel so prestigious."

"It's a shame people don't respect historical buildings as much as they should. Luckily, the outside appears well preserved," I said as we turned back towards the crossing.

"I guess it's all about money."

"These days, everything is about money." Even a family's love.

As we approached the MCG the jostling crowd became thicker. In a split-second, Evie and I were separated. After we made our way back to each other, I clasped her hand. I liked its warmth and how holding it made me feel connected to her. This type of intimacy was missing from my last few relationships—not that you could even call them relationships. For the girls, our relationship had been more about looks, status, and money, leaving my heart empty.

The last time I dated was over twelve months ago. I had been seeing Tatiana for a couple of months. I thought she was different from the usual money-hungry girls I attracted. She wasn't obsessed with social media or taking selfies or plastic surgery or enhancing everything God gave her. She seemed more reserved, more natural. But as time went on, she showed her true colors. One evening we went out to a restaurant of her choice. One of the upmarket ones, of course. I would have been happy with tacos.

When the waiter asked for our wine order, she snatched the menu from me and ordered the most expensive. She probably didn't even know what it was, or what it tasted like; all she did was look at the price tag. Her phone rang, and she answered it right there in the middle of dinner. She got up to go to the bathroom, still talking on her phone. I heard her say, "He might be good to look at, but he's boring. Lucky he has money."

Her callous words felt like a slap in the face. I got up and left, giving the bottle of wine to the waiter, telling him to enjoy it. I'd given up on finding someone after that.

Evie was different. She spoke to people today while we were walking the dogs. She listened to them, smiled at them, though she had nothing to gain from it. Her friendships were genuine. People liked her. And she liked nature. I liked nature. I guess that's one of the things Tatiana found boring about me. I was happy to walk in nature or surf or learn about animals. She was more into fine dining and being seen in the right scene.

As soon as we were out of the crowd, Evie let go of my hand.

Evie and I met the others at an entry gate to collect our tickets from Jonas before we made our way to our seats. We were on the second level in the center of the ground — a good position to be in.

"What do you know about cricket?" Evie asked.

"Nothing. I've never watched it before."

"You didn't google it?"

"No. Sometimes I prefer to learn about things like a normal person. I don't want to get bogged down in all the details and statistics. It's not as much fun," I said so only she could hear.

"Ok. Let me explain it then," she said. "So, you know the rules of baseball, right?"

"Yes."

"Well, it's nothing like that," she said, a smile lighting her face.

CHAPTER FIVE

EVIE

JESSE HAD DECIDED he would like to help me again. He said he'd checked the weather last night and found the surf wouldn't be favourable that day, so I agreed. There was no harm in him joining me. I liked his company. His hiking stories were interesting.

"We have more time today, so I can take you through your induction and training," I said to Jesse as we got out of the car. "Do you know much about dogs?"

"Not really. I didn't have any pets growing up."

I nodded. No pets. What a depressing childhood. Some of my best friends were animals.

"OK. Broadly speaking, you have happy dogs, scared dogs, and aggressive dogs. We won't work with aggressive dogs. I don't want any walkers injured. So, I meet with owners to determine what their needs are and check out the dog's temperament before I agree to take them on as clients."

Jesse nodded.

Upstairs, I opened an apartment door, and Jesse followed me in. Mindy, a lanky, growing-into-herself pit bull came bounding towards us. Jesse's eyes widened, and he took a step back. Mindy didn't notice him. She made a beeline for me, skidding to a stop at my feet, wagging her tail so hard her whole body moved in response.

"Mindy is a friendly dog. She's young and has lots of energy to burn. If she were to jump up at me now, I would say no in a firm voice. If that didn't stop her, I'd lift my knee into her chest to push her away. It wouldn't hurt her, but it'd stop her from jumping on me and possibly hurting me."

"OK," Jesse said, as I gave Mindy a pat for being a good girl.

"OK. You're going to introduce yourself now. Always approach slowly, so the dog isn't startled, and use a calm voice to let them know you are approaching. Do not approach from the front. It's confronting for some dogs. It's best to approach from the side. Some dogs find it threatening if you look them in the eye, so focus somewhere else. Their chest is a good option."

He followed my instructions to the letter, looking up at me periodically for reassurance. I nodded and smiled. He wasn't cocky. He didn't act like he knew everything. If he was unsure, he would ask. I liked that.

"Hold your hand out in a fist and let her smell you. See how she's having a good sniff and is wagging her tail? That means you can give her a pat. The best place to pat when you first meet is the shoulder, chest, or neck. Yep, that's excellent. We don't go for the head first, because they can feel threatened. Just like when we meet someone, we don't want them patting our cheek; a handshake is just fine."

He patted her side. She leaned into him, nearly pushing him over. Instead of standing in anger or pushing her away, he braced himself, so he was better balanced and continued patting. I smiled inwardly at his kindness.

"If she were scared, we would take extra care to make sure our voice is soft and calm. It would be good to crouch next to her, so she feels less threatened. If she moved away from you, if her tail was tucked in or she was looking at you from the sides of her eyes, it would be best not to pat her. We wouldn't want to stress her out. Scared dogs can become aggressive."

I knew I could give these instructions to Jesse in one go because he would be able to remember them. Other people I would have trained over a couple of sessions.

Jesse continued to rub Mindy vigorously. Her tongue lolled, and she dropped to the floor, asking for belly rubs. For someone who knew nothing about dogs, it was impressive how he connected with just one touch.

"Mindy likes to go for a run on our walks. Before we run with a dog, we make sure it has basic obedience skills and is listening. Are you OK with running?" I asked him.

"Yeah. I run a couple of times a week."

"That's lucky. I hated running until I found out some of the dogs love it. I had to train myself physically and mentally. What they like will be noted on their profile on the app."

We left the apartment block and walked for a bit. I made sure Mindy stopped when I asked her to and listened to my instructions. I went through the process with Jesse as we made our way to a nearby park.

"Ready?"

"Yep."

I took off with Jesse by my side. Mindy tagged along at first and then started to speed up and take the lead. She was extra excited today. She kept turning to look between Jesse and me. I sped up to match her. She ran even faster. There was no way I could keep up.

I tugged on her lead. Firmly, I said, "Mindy, walk."

But even though I slowed my feet, Mindy didn't slow hers. I was concentrating so hard on not falling on my face, I barely noticed Jesse, who was keeping pace beside me.

Without warning, Mindy changed direction, running right in front of us. I saw what was going to happen, but I couldn't stop it. Jesse tried to dodge her, but she took his legs out from underneath him. He flew in front of me, like Superman, arms and legs outstretched. I tried to dodge him. But Mindy circled me, tripping me up with the lead, and I followed Jesse to the ground. Except I didn't actually hit the ground. Instead, I landed on top of Jesse.

CHAPTER SIX

JESSE

THE AIR WAS KNOCKED out of me as Evie landed on top of me unceremoniously. I felt her jerk as Mindy tried to keep running in whichever direction took her fancy. With her arm being pulled over my head, I could see she had a firm hold on the lead.

Mindy stopped and looked back at both of us. She cocked her head to the side, probably wondering what we were doing lying on the grass. As she came back to us, I felt Evie relax on top of me. That was until Mindy reached us and started layering us with slobbery dog kisses. Evie buried her head in my back while she begged Mindy to stop. She was laughing so hard at her failed attempts to stop Mindy that as she tried to get up, she collapsed back on top of me. I tried not to laugh, because each time I did, I got a mouthful of grass.

Then Evie's weight lifted off me as she pulled herself to her feet. I rolled over and found she was standing above me. Our eyes met. The intimacy of the eye contact threw me, and my stomach knotted as I gazed up at her. Her flushed face beamed down at me.

My eyes were glued to her. Her polo shirt didn't betray the curves underneath, but that didn't stop me from thinking about her soft breasts that only moments before had been pressed against my back. What if I had landed on my back instead? How would it have felt, being that close to her, face to face?

She shifted her weight from one foot to the other, dragging me up out of my thoughts. Reluctantly, I drew my eyes away, back to her face. She peered down at me, the intensity tightened my chest. My heart thumped, sending tingles through my veins.

She tore her eyes away from mine.

"And that is how it's done," she said emphatically, pulling Mindy away so I could get up with some dignity. I was covered in cut grass, and I was sure I must have had a grass stain on my face.

"So, what you're saying is I need to find some poor unsuspecting soul to cushion my fall? Making sure I mash their face into the ground and use them as a shield against a tongue wielding dog?" I said, looking at her with raised eyebrows.

"Yeah, that will work," she said, smiling. Then, as she took in the rest of me, her face became somber. "Oh, Jesse, I'm so sorry. Are you OK?"

Still holding onto Mindy's leash, she approached me and started wiping the grass off my shirt. Her smile disappeared as she apologized repeatedly. Her hands were shaking. When she looked at me, her eyes were unfocused, and she looked away, almost fearful.

"Evie, it's OK. It was an accident. Mindy was just too excited."

She nodded almost imperceptibly.

"At least we can entertain everyone tonight with a good story after the movies."

WE ALL MET at the movie theatre. My eyes searched for Evie and found her almost instantly. Her long brown hair cascaded down her back. She was wearing skin-tight jeans, showing off her amazing curves. Her crop top exposed some of her olive skin above the waistband of her jeans. My eyes made their way over her breasts, the tops of which peaked out the top of her shirt, before reaching her face.

She was watching me. Shit, talk about being caught. Again. Grinning, I made my way toward her.

"Let's go to the candy bar," Evie said after we'd all bought tickets. She was back to her normal, relaxed self. I wondered at her reaction this afternoon – she'd barely looked at me for the rest of the day and had apologized more than once.

I watched as she ordered a bucket of popcorn, a large drink, and ice cream. My eyes bulged out of my head at the amount of food she had. She wasn't one to pick at salads or only consume shakes. Her food was as real as she was.

When she looked at me, she raised her eyebrows and shrugged. "What? You look like a stunned mullet. Don't American girls eat this much?"

"I'm impressed you can eat all that and still look so good. Dare I ask what a stunned mullet is?"

Jonas draped his arm around my shoulder, laughing. "You know when you catch a fish and knock it out? And its eyes goggle at you and its mouth hangs open? Well, that's what we call a stunned mullet. You are doing a perfect impersonation."

"OK. Got it. I'll stick my eyes back in now," I said, joining in the laughter.

We made our way to the theatre with Evie trailing at the end. When we got to our row, I entered first. Everyone else conspicuously waited for Evie to enter next before following.

Evie and I shared the arm rest. I liked how her warmth seeped through me where our arms touched. All of a sudden, she yelped when the actress on-screen opened a door, and her date was unexpectedly waiting on the other side. It was an innocuous scene. I don't think anyone else in the theatre got a fright. She must have realized the same because just as unforeseen as her yelp was, the laughter that came next was surprising. She didn't seem able to control herself. She bent over double, trying to keep her laughter in, her breathing coming rapidly. I couldn't help but smile and gave her back a quick rub. She became rigid under my touch. I removed my hand immediately.

When she sat up, tears were glistening in her eyes. I was unsure if it was because of the uncontrolled laughter or my touch. My stomach dropped.

"HAVE you noticed Evie gets tense and jumpy sometimes?" I asked Jonas as we went to the bar to buy a round of drinks after the movie.

"When we first met her, she was really bad, almost jumping at shadows. I hardly see it now. Maybe it's because you're new, and she's still getting to know you."

"Maybe."

"She doesn't talk about her ex, Nick. But he must have been a real piece of work. When we first met her, she didn't enjoy interacting much. She kept her head down and hardly talked. And she would always apologize if things went wrong, like we were going to get angry with her or something."

We returned to the group. Evie had started telling them about the incident with Mindy. I moved closer to her, trying to draw her attention to me.

She looked at me, smiling as I handed her a beer. I felt like she was gauging my reaction, making sure it was OK to tell the story.

CHAPTER SEVEN

EVIE

I SMILED at Jesse as he moved in close to me.

Jesse, who didn't get angry with me this afternoon after our accident. I'd expected him to. I was afraid of his reaction, but he hadn't yelled or called me names. Instead, he'd reassured me it was OK and laughed it off. I'd seen how kind he was to Mindy afterwards. He hadn't scolded her once. He'd given her a pat and told her she was a good girl before graciously accepting a kiss from her.

Jesse, who, in the movie theatre when I'd lost control, hadn't grabbed my arm and pinched it because I was embarrassing him. He did not whisper menacingly in my ear to shut up while twisting the pinch so viciously it would have taken all my power not to cry out in pain. Instead, he'd given my back a quick rub, and when I'd looked at him, asked if I was OK.

The first time I'd embarrassed Nick, we were with a group of his friends. We were in a beer garden, and the paving was uneven. I laughed at a joke and lost my footing. I reached out to a guy next to me to steady myself, and in the process, I spilt my drink on Nick. His friends laughed it off, but Nick didn't think it was funny. His hand had gripped my arm so tight his fingers latched around my bone, digging in with such force I thought the muscle was going to tear away.

I had been scared. I didn't make eye contact with him for the rest of the night. When we got home, he let the door close behind us before grabbing me by the throat and slamming me against the wall. Only the tips of my toes touched the ground.

The force of his hand around my windpipe stopped my airflow. Blackness creeped into the corners of my eyes, and my brain barely registered the words as he told me if I embarrassed him again, he would crush me. I tried to bat his hand away. My strength disappeared as the air trapped in my lungs suffocated me. He let go, and I collapsed to the floor. I avoided going out with him as much as I could after that.

Now, I checked Jesse's demeanour. He was not tense. His eyes didn't threaten. He was turned towards me, open. I wanted to step in closer to him to feel his warmth. To touch him ever so slightly, so the little spark of electricity I felt could be intensified. My fingers twitched. I forced restraint.

"It's such a shame it wasn't caught on camera," Jesse said, laughing. "Mindy was too excited for her own good. One minute we were running along, me thinking about the hot girl running next to me. Next thing you know, I was flying through the air..."

"He looked like Superman, just less super," I said, laughing hard, taking hold of his arm.

"I hit the ground hard, the momentum sliding me along. Then, without warning, Evie lands on top of me."

"Mindy turns around and looks at us like, 'What are you humans doing?'"

"The look on her face was hilarious. She looked between Evie and me with her head cocked. Then out of nowhere, this big grin emerges."

"I shit you not. She has a prize-winning smile on her face as she comes up with a new game in her head."

I look at Jesse, who was cringing and laughing at the same time.

He continued our story, "And this traitor was lying on top of me, trapping me. She buried her face in my back, leaving me wide open to big, fat, slobbery dog kisses."

"I'm sorry," I say, trying to sound apologetic.

"Sure, you are," he said, not taking his smiling eyes off my face.

At that moment, I took in every feature of his face wholly and completely. His full lips that were always ready to smile. Would they be soft to kiss? His sparkling blue eyes and how they crinkled when he laughed, remembering the furrow between them when he thought about some random thing I'd said. His thick brown hair pushed up out of his face, and highlights which reminded me of rich toffee, which I'd never noticed before. I liked what I saw, and it worried me. But what worried me more was the way I was starting to feel. The pull I felt towards him.

Miranda interrupted my thoughts. "I'm glad you two had a good day bonding over dog slobber."

I joined in their laughter as they discussed in detail how disgusting dog slobber was. When I snuck a look at Jesse, I found him looking at me, smiling.

I felt butterflies in my stomach as I averted my eyes, blushing.

"How about we go to the zoo on Saturday? We haven't been there for ages," Jonas said.

"I'm in," Jesse said enthusiastically. "I'd love to see more Australian animals. Do they have drop bears?"

"Sure do," Miranda said, stifling a giggle.

Jesse. Drop bears. I would have to tell him. What would his reaction be? Would he be angry?

CHAPTER EIGHT

JESSE

AS WE WALKED towards the zoo gates, Evie took hold of my arm, slowing me down. She leant towards me and said quietly, "Jesse, drop bears aren't real. It's OK for us to have a joke with you about it, but I don't want you to be embarrassed if someone here says something to you."

At times, it seemed like fear ran through her veins. I saw it in her face when uncertainty took over. Yet, she was brave enough to tell me they were playing a joke on me. She may have been scared of what my reaction would be, but took a risk and told me anyway.

"I know," I said.

Her head jerked back, and she studied my face. "What? Are you playing us?"

"I wanted to see how long all of you would keep up the charade for."

She smiled, her eyes twinkling as she pulled me toward the others. When she let go of my arm, the place her hand had been felt cold. I wanted to grab her hand, to hold it in mine, to feel close to her. But I was worried she would withdraw hers and shut me out. She had shown no interest in me other than friendliness.

"We should go see the drop bears first," said Evie.

"True. They become less active as the day warms up," Georgia said, pushing her long blond hair over her shoulder.

We followed them to the Australian animal habitat. A smile played at Evie's lips. I wondered what she was up to. Jonas led us through an open area where kangaroos roamed freely. Some approached humans for a snack. Others lay in the shade, not taking any notice of the world around them.

"The drop bears are over this way," Jonas said, offering a sneaky smile to his sister.

We followed as he spoke non-stop about drop bears. The others joined in, adding details, just as they had on our hike. Evie took my hand as she slowed her pace and held a finger to her lips. The distance between us and the front group increased. They were so absorbed in the story they were telling they didn't even notice. Evie turned us around and took off at a run, laughing, still holding my hand.

"I wonder how long until they notice us missing," I said, laughing along with her.

We made our way back past the nonchalant kangaroos, and out of the Australian animal area before Evie got a text from Georgia. *Where are you?*

Evie let go of my hand. Mine felt empty, like it was missing something.

Taking a walk. We'll meet you for lunch at the café at one.

"Where are we going?" I asked her.

"Wherever you like. It's your day."

"I would like to see the seal keeper talk. I love seals. They're like the puppies of the ocean."

"Why don't we do a seal close-up before the talk? Get to see them and meet with them?"

"Could we? Really?"

She smiled and nodded.

As we walked toward the seal enclosure, I took hold of her hand again. If she pulled away, I would take that as a signal that I was going too fast for her. I needed to take this at her pace. I would let her actions guide me. Her hand stayed in mine.

It was exciting to get close to the seals and watch their antics. When the seal waved her fin, it was with such gusto her whole body swayed.

"She's like Mindy," Evie said to me, smiling widely.

I nodded. My smile matched hers.

I'd spent every day that week working with Evie. We'd walked Mindy twice, and she was full of energy and happy, happy, happy. And she gave us her prize-winning smile. I always thought pit bulls were aggressive. But Mindy proved me wrong. Evie taught me it wasn't the dog, but usually, the owner who caused the aggressive behavior.

The seal gave us a smile when we patted her. We experienced her fishy breath firsthand when she gave us each a kiss. Thinking it was a perfect opportunity, I leant over and gave Evie a kiss on the cheek and thanked her.

WHEN WE ARRIVED AT LUNCH, Georgia looked up at us and smiled. They had chosen a table with a great vantage point opposite the giraffe enclosure.

"Good job ditching us. We turned around, and you had disappeared. In your spot was a group of tourists wanting to see an elusive drop bear."

Evie and I smiled at each other.

"Serves you right for telling stories," Evie said.

"Where did you go?" Jonas asked, as Evie and I sat down next to each other.

"We went to see the seals," Evie said.

"We didn't just see them. We met one. It was the best thing. She was so darn cute."

"Who? Evie or the seal?" Miranda asked.

Evie shifted in her chair.

"Both. And she gave us a kiss," I said, trying to make it less awkward.

"Who? Evie or the seal?" Georgia asked, giving me a wink.

"Oh, for goodness sake, the seal gave us a kiss," Evie said, rolling her eyes. She deliberately bit into her BBQ Kransky, Australian for Polish sausage, as if trying to put an end to the conversation.

"Hey, the oldies are having a barbie in a couple of weeks. Do you want to come?" Jonas asked.

I looked at Evie blankly. I had no idea what he'd said.

"Their parents are having a BBQ. Would you like to go?"

"Oh, OK. Yes."

"Bring your bathers. No budgie smugglers allowed, though."

What? I looked at Evie again.

"They have a pool. So, bring swimwear. But not speedos."

"Speedos are budgie smugglers? Budgie as in the bird?"

Everyone laughed.

"Yes, the lump in the front looks like a budgie has been shoved down there," Evie explained.

"And you know that how? Because people shove birds in their speedos?"

"We don't know how we know, we just know," Jonas said.

Yeah, because that made so much sense.

"Do you want us to bring anything?" Evie asked.

"If you can drop into the Bottle-O on the way and grab a slab of coldies, that would be great," Jonas said.

"Are you guys even talking English?" I asked.

They laughed heartily at my apparent lack of Australian speak.

"They want us to go to the bottle shop...wait, you'd call it a liquor store, to buy a carton of beer."

"Right."

That made them laugh even harder.

"They live out woop woop, so we'll organize some beds for you."

Evie didn't even wait for me to ask this time.

"They live out in the middle of nowhere, in the country."

CHAPTER NINE

EVIE

JESSE WAS at Bells Beach today, surfing, which meant I was working alone. I found it strange driving to work without him in the car. Some days we'd be stuck in traffic for over an hour, and we would chat, listen to the radio, laugh at the morning presenters, and sing along to the songs.

As I walked the dogs, I found my mind wandering.

Yesterday, Jesse commented on how friendly I was. I wasn't always. When I was growing up, I was quiet. I didn't want to say anything wrong. Most things I *said* were frowned upon by my parents. Most things I *did* were frowned upon by my parents. I was shy and reserved, trying to protect myself from their disdain.

After Nick, I'd decided to try a new approach. I forced myself out of my comfort zone. It took a lot of practice to look at people and give them a smile. When they said hello, I learnt to say hello back. Slowly, I became comfortable having conversations with them. I saw how it made them feel important to have someone to talk to, to listen to them. I started doing it more. I didn't share myself with other people, not more than I had to. But I liked talking to them.

I noticed Jesse was the same. He would stop and talk to the people we regularly saw. It wasn't just a pose. He remembered things about them. He asked questions. He was genuinely interested. I also noticed how the conversation was usually not directed towards him. He felt more comfortable talking about them. I wondered why.

At lunch time, my phone beeped. My heart gave a little flutter when I thought it might be Jesse. When I saw Jonas's name, my heart sank.

What the hell was I thinking? There was no place in my life for a man or a relationship. I was happy. I didn't need anyone to destroy my happiness. I didn't need anyone like Nick. How could I ever trust anyone after Nick?

And who said Jesse liked me like that anyway? Holding hands didn't have to mean anything. Just because I sometimes caught him glancing at me, it didn't mean anything. Just because he smiled and laughed along with me, it didn't mean anything. Just because he complimented me, it didn't mean anything. It felt like he enjoyed my company, but I could say exactly the same things about Jonas. And we were just friends.

And besides, he would probably be leaving soon.

This line of thought was stupid and dangerous. It had to stop.

I accepted Jonas's invitation to pizza night and got back to walking the dogs.

BEFORE HEADING HOME, I dropped into the cat rescue. I needed to do some soul searching, and what better place to do it than with my beautiful cat friends. I headed straight to Mike's enclosure and gave him a pat as I entered.

He was my trusty friend who would always listen in my time of need.

I sat and leant against the wall; my legs spread out in front of me. I pulled up Harry Potter on my phone and started to read. Sally came over and stretched her sleek body against my leg. I patted her distractedly. Long, languid pats, the type she enjoyed the most.

When Mike came over, he stretched his nose to the hand holding my phone. He nuzzled it purposefully, his nose wet and his purrs loud. His nuzzles became more intense, so much so, I could no longer read. I put the phone down and caressed his head. He pushed his head into my hand, moving it up and down, his purrs becoming louder. I smiled down at him. It was like he knew I was there to speak.

"I don't know, Mike. What do you think? Do you think Jesse's a good guy?"

He stopped his head-rubbing and looked at me with his expressive, knowing eyes. He gave my hand a nudge. I caressed his ears.

"Yeah, I know you do. You are always happy to see him. You pay him nearly as much attention as you do me."

Mike rolled onto his back, taking my hand with him. I continued massaging his ears. What was I supposed to do? Trust the instincts of a cat? They were probably better than my instincts. He wouldn't be led astray by a weak heart. Or a muddled mind.

I smiled down at Mike.

"Yes, you're right."

A content smile spread across his face as he closed his eyes and went to sleep. I sat there and patted him and Sally until it was time to leave.

I WALKED through the iron gate of the rented house I called home. It was nothing fancy, but I loved the character. Lining the fence were rose bushes, probably as old as the house itself. In early summer, their blooms of pink and white emitted a lovely perfume.

Beyond the tiny garden stood the single-fronted house. The façade was rendered in white. On the little porch sat a bench seat, a lovely spot to sit on warm evenings, and watch the sun set over the rooftops of nearly identical houses across the street.

I opened the black wooden door and followed the long corridor, stretching along one side of the house to the living area at the back. The bifold wooden and glass doors led out to a brick paved terrace.

I remembered how, when I first moved to the house, the expanse and emptiness scared me. It was a tiny house, two bedrooms, a bathroom, kitchen, and living area. But it felt huge compared to the single room I'd lived in for weeks. At first, I slept with all of the lights on, as if the brightness could protect me. Slowly, I filled the house with second-hand furniture. As the weeks and months passed, the house felt like it was a part of me. I turned the lights off at night, room by room, until the day I found I could walk through the house in darkness and not feel an ounce of fear.

I sat on the couch and looked out at the sunny terrace. My phone beeped beside me.

Cleopatra.

It was our—Shane's and my—secret password, the one we used to know if it was safe to call. He was my oldest friend, the only one who knew me, my past.

I replied.

Ruled

The phone rang.

"Hi, Shane."

"Evie darling, how are you?"

His soft-lilted voice made me smile.

"Great. How about you?"

I lay down on the couch.

"Nothing has changed."

"Still waiting for a sexy man to walk into your life and sweep you off your feet?" I teased.

"Of course."

"You know, they don't just drop out of the sky. You need to be an active single. Go out. Meet some people."

"Yeah, yeah, I know. I took your advice and joined a local gay club. They have regular wine tasting nights. At least if they are dead-shit boring, I can get sloshed, and it won't be a total waste."

"You crack me up. You remind me of Georgia and Miranda."

"I should come for a visit. They sound like my kind of people."

"You should."

I fell silent as I realised what I'd said. Shane had been to visit a couple of times since I'd escaped. But I always tried to keep my old life separate from my new. I wasn't ashamed of what had happened to me, but I felt like it shouldn't muddy my new life. But that was stupid. What happened to me changed me and already affected my friendships and decisions. No matter how much I tried to hold it at arms-length, it infiltrated anyway. I didn't want Shane, my closest friend in the world, the man who knew my deepest secrets, my saviour, to feel like he wasn't a part of my life.

"Evie?"

"Yeah."

"What's going on?"

"Nothing."

I'd answered way too quickly for it not to be suspicious.

"You've never wanted me to be a part of your new life. I don't mind. I know you do it to protect yourself."

"I don't want you to be an extra in my life, Shane. I have kept you apart for too long."

"That makes me the happiest man in the world."

I felt a warm glow at the honesty in his statement.

"I'm sorry it took me so long."

"The length of time doesn't matter to me, Evie. The fact that you are strong enough now to let your past meet your future makes me proud."

Time for some more honesty. I sat up and moved myself to the edge of the seat. The force of what I was about to say caused me to press the balls of my feet into the ground.

"I've met someone."

Shane waited for me to continue.

"I didn't think I'd ever want to be in another relationship, and I'm not saying I want to now, but Jesse is different. I'm scared. What if it's all an act? What if he is just manipulating me with niceness?"

"Do you think he is?"

"No."

"Just take it slow. Trust your instincts. You're a different person now, Evie. Listen to your gut."

"Everything tells me he is different from Nick. But what if I'm just fooling myself?"

"Evie, there are good people in the world. If you think Jesse is one, then he probably is."

I stared out the window, looking at the potted geraniums, one by one. Could I be strong enough to let Jesse in?

"What do your friends think of him?"

"They think he's nice. They're encouraging me."

"I'm sure they're right."

"But he's from America, and only here for a holiday. What's the point of starting something if he's just going to leave?"

"Stop rushing to the end. Enjoy your time with him, learn about each other. If it leads to it, discover what it's like to be in love."

I nodded, even though Shane couldn't see.

"Your past will make you wary, but you can still be open to new possibilities."

"Yes, you're right. Just because I like someone, it doesn't mean it's forever."

"That's my girl."

"Thanks, Shane."

"I'll call you next month."

"OK."

Now, I had Mike and Shane telling me the same thing.

"I LOVE how you have your own pizza oven so you can make us all pizzas," I said to Jonas as I handed him a beer.

The smell of pizza made my stomach rumble.

"Better than store bought pizza any day," Georgia said.

"For sure."

We sat around the fire pit while Jonas worked his magic, moving the pizzas around the oven. The garden was completely different from my paved terrace. The fire pit and pizza oven were set off to one side amongst lawn that was so lush it was like a living carpet beneath your feet. Garden beds lined the fences filled with plants of heights and colours so vastly different it created a feeling of depth. Serenity in suburbia is what I called it.

The doorbell rang, and Miranda got up to answer it. When she walked into the backyard with Jesse, my heart gave a little lurch. He was wearing jeans, and I couldn't help but notice how well they hugged his butt. He looked around the group, and when he spotted me, he smiled and made a beeline for me.

He sat close to me, our legs touching. His warmth spread through me and settled in my stomach — a ball of contentment.

"How was your day?" he asked.

"Good. How was the surf?"

"It was amazing. Bells Beach has some really nice swells and breaks. Was Benny feeling better today?"

I smiled inwardly. He knew I was worried about Benny. Jesse was thoughtful. I wasn't used to that. Nick wouldn't have cared if the dog was dying at his feet as long as it didn't make a mess.

"Not really. I put him in the backpack and took him for a short walk."

"I'll bet he liked that."

"Mindy was disappointed when you didn't come through the door with me—"

"Hey, you two, there are more than just the two of you here, you know. How about you ask us how our day was?" Georgia teased.

I blushed and turned back towards the group.

"Georgia, how was your day?" Jesse asked.

"Well, now that you ask, I had a lovely day at the office."

I rolled my eyes at her.

"Jesse, we have Hawaiian, the lot, Aussie, meat galore and cheese pizza. What would you like?" Jonas asked.

"I'll try the Aussie and meat galore, please."

"Your wish is my command."

When the plate was handed to him, he openly stared at it. "Egg and bacon pizza. That's interesting."

We all watched him while he took his first bite. He chewed slowly.

"Mmm, that's good."

"Ah, so he has good taste in pizza and in girls," Miranda said, giving Jesse a wink.

Jesse smiled. He looked at me and said, "I think they're talking about you."

"I thought they were talking about Mindy," I replied, trying to make it sound light-hearted.

"What movie are we watching tonight?" Georgia asked.

"Movie?" Jesse asked me.

"They set up a big screen outside. We sit around the fire pit and watch a movie once it's dark enough."

"Cool."

"Jesse can choose, seeing it's his first visit," Jonas said.

Jesse nodded his head eagerly. I couldn't wait to hear what he came up with.

"*Zombieland.*"

"OMG. Yes, the double tap," Miranda said gleefully.

We cleared away and brought the beanbags out onto the lawn. There were only four, which meant we needed to share. I sat on the bag next to Jesse, trying not to sit too close, but it was impossible not to in a beanbag.

As the movie started, Jesse reached over and took my hand. I felt butterflies in my stomach. The night air started to cool, and I moved in closer to him, relishing in the sparks where our skin touched. It was a nice feeling being close to someone, enjoying their space. One side of my brain was saying it was nice, the other side was saying it wasn't a good idea to get that close.

Zombieland, Rule Number Thirty-two, enjoy the little things.

CHAPTER TEN

JESSE

THE MORE TIME I spent with Evie, the more time I wanted to spend with her. She was like a packet of cookies where you couldn't stop at eating just one. But it was hard to tell what she was thinking. Last night we'd held hands watching the movie, and she'd moved in closer to me. I hoped she was starting to feel what I was feeling.

But when we walked to the pub for lunch after we'd done our duties at the rescue, she did not walk with me, even though Jonas, Miranda, and Georgia did. I tried to tell myself it was because she wanted to speak to the other volunteers, and it wasn't because she was deliberately avoiding me.

I longed to hold her hand again, to feel her skin against mine.

When she sat down next to me at the table, I rested my hand on her leg. She didn't tense up like she had the first time I did it. There was a lightness in my heart at the realization.

"Are you having the steak again?" I asked her, giving her a smile.

"No," she said flatly.

"Oh, OK, I thought it was your favorite protein."

"Am I that predictable? You think I can't have something different for a change?" she asked with an unusual harshness to her voice.

When she looked at me, her jaw was tense, and her eyes fierce. I took my hand off her leg. I stared down at the table. She moved her body away from me, shutting me out. What had I done to upset her?

She got up abruptly and said, "I'm going to order."

I sat there, not knowing whether to follow her. I didn't want to upset her by doing the wrong thing. But maybe if we were away from the table, I could ask what was wrong. Maybe if she bit my head off, it would hurt a little less if we weren't surrounded by people.

I joined her in line. She didn't acknowledge my presence.

"I'm sorry I upset you."

She didn't say a word. Didn't look at me. Her shoulders remained stiff.

"What did I say?"

"I don't need you to tell me what I like and don't like," she snapped.

I reeled at her accusation. That was not what I had meant to do at all. I wanted to protest but was afraid it would just make it worse. She continued to avoid looking at me, and I continued to stand there. I needed to say something.

"That's not what I meant to do," I said to her.

She stood so taut that if she were a string on a violin, she would snap if plucked. I touched her arm gently. She whirled around, moving out of my reach, and glared at me. I took a step backwards, involuntarily. When she looked at my face, hers softened. Tears sprang into her eyes.

She left the line and walked out to the beer garden. I followed her out.

"Leave me alone, Jesse. I just want to be alone."

I didn't think that was true, but maybe I was wrong. Everything she was doing confused me. She was so hot and cold. Last night I thought she was warming up to me, the chemical reaction slow but steady, like slow combustion. Today she was like the ice queen, icicles shooting from her eyes and piercing my skin.

I had spent my whole life backing away when my parents were angry at me. I couldn't keep doing that. I needed to take action. I couldn't keep living the same pattern. Tentatively, I moved closer, trying to see if she would respond. If she didn't, if she was adamant that I leave, then I would. I braced myself.

"Evie," I said softly as I approached her. She was only a couple of steps away, but it felt like an abyss. I moved slowly, so I didn't startle her, as if she were an injured or frightened animal. She looked everywhere but at me. As I got closer, she took a small step back before raising her eyes to mine.

Tears rolled down her cheeks. I took a small step towards her and held out my hand. When she didn't shy away from it, I touched her arm. Her shoulders sagged, and her body shuddered as she tried to control her tears.

"I'm sorry, Jesse. You didn't do anything wrong."

"OK." I didn't want to push her and hoped she would continue.

"It reminded me of Nick. He never let me think for myself."

"That's not what I was trying to do." I moved closer and rubbed her arm.

"I know."

I wrapped her in my arms and held her while she cried. What had Nick done to her? How could memories two years later still affect her so deeply? She let me hold her. My arms tightened, and I kissed the top of her head.

AS I WALKED into my apartment that afternoon, I called April, my best friend back home. The apartment was really a loft above a garage in a leafy suburb. It was exactly what I needed. Fully furnished, one bedroom, modern and comfortable. The owners of the house were in their late twenties with two young children. They invited me to dinner at least twice a week, and I enjoyed those evenings, feeling I was a part of something bigger than just myself.

April answered as I kicked off my shoes and stretched my legs out on the chaise. I imagined her sitting cross-legged on one of her colorful floor cushions in front of the TV. She would be starting her stretches before bed soon.

"Hello."

"Hi, April."

"Jesse, how is everything?"

"Good, Melbourne is beautiful. It's a big city, but the people are friendly."

"Have you made some friends?"

"Yeah, I hang out with a couple of guys when I head out surfing. And there's a group of people from the cat shelter I enjoy spending time with."

One in particular.

"Is it true what they say about the weather? Four seasons in one day?"

She had me on loudspeaker and I could hear her shifting around, getting into different stretch positions.

"Have you been doing some Googling?" I asked, surprised at her knowledge.

"I wanted to know what it was like."

Her voice was drawn out as if it was mimicking her stretch.

"The weather is exactly like that sometimes. You can be as hot as hell, and then a storm rolls in, and you have to scurry for warm clothes."

"Well, at least it's not boring. What have you been up to?"

"Not much different from the last time we spoke."

I didn't want to tell her about Evie yet. I wanted to enjoy Evie for myself for a while and see how it all worked out. April was my closest friend in the world. She was my first true friend since Susie-May. My mother had tried to drive a wedge between us, but I was a different person when April and I met. I was no longer a teenager, reliant on my parents. I was stronger. April was defiant, too, and she did not back down.

The night we met, I was walking down North Western Avenue in Los Angeles, after having dinner at a Mexican grill. April approached me from a side street, wearing a short skirt and an even shorter top, giving me a faint smile.

"Hi there, sexy. Would you like to get a room?"

She looked anywhere but at my face, twisting her hands. Finally, she raised her eyes to mine.

"Is that what you really want to do?" I asked, staring straight into her deep brown eyes.

"Not really, but a girl's gotta eat."

"Why don't we go grab a meal instead, then?"

I wanted her to look at me to see I was genuine. I didn't need to be propositioned by a prostitute on the side of the road, one who was obviously new to all of this. She didn't fit the mold. But I guess none of them did to start with.

Biting her lip, she looked up at me. I attempted my most reassuring smile. Smiling back, she gave me a small nod.

"OK."

We went to a diner close by. I ordered a soda for myself and told her to order whatever she wanted.

"You're not going to eat?" she asked, her eyes narrowing.

"No, I've already eaten."

"This is not some kind of strange fetish, is it?"

I laughed. I liked her openness and honesty.

"No, but I can order fries if that would make you feel better."

"Well, it would be better than you watching me eat."

I ordered fries.

"I'm Jesse. What's your name?"

"April."

"How long have you been doing this?"

"A couple of nights. I've been living in my car. I was getting food vouchers and stuff, but they ran out a week ago."

"Why are you living in your car?"

"My parents kicked me out of the house. They found out I was bisexual, and they're super religious. I moved all the way across the country to get away from them and their hate. I thought I could get a fresh start in a place where I knew no one."

I didn't know what to say to that, so we sat in silence until our food arrived. I sat there looking at her. Her dark eyes reminded me of a deer when you came across it while walking in the wilderness. Startled. Aware. She stared right back.

"Sounds to me like you need a job and a place to stay."

"It's hard to find a job with no address, and it's hard to find a place to live with no job."

"What skills do you have?"

"I've completed my organizational psychology degree."

I gazed at her while running my hand across my jaw.

"That's interesting. I could use the services of someone like you." The words had come out before I really thought about them.

Her eyes widened. "Really?"

"Yes, I think your skills can improve my business."

"And what business is that?" she asked, tilting her head, studying me closely.

"I own a share trading firm."

"And how could you use my skills, exactly?"

"To help my workers."

I didn't know right then just how much of an asset April would be to my business. She had been invaluable to both my workers and me. She helped with their decision-making ability and wellness, which in turn, helped me.

"I have a spare room in my apartment. You can stay there while you get back on your feet."

"And what do you expect in return?"

Again, that honesty pleased me.

"That you do a good job and look out for me."

"No kinky business?"

"No."

And so began our friendship. She supported me in everything. Even when I said I was sick of going through the motions every day, that I wanted to go somewhere where I was completely unknown, to find what made me happy, to find balance, she supported me without question.

I was pulled back into the present as April said, "Jesse?"

"Yeah, sorry. I was waiting for you to finish your stretch."

"All finished now. How much longer are you staying there?"

"I'm not sure yet. I've got lots to see and do."

"I bet."

"I'll let you get to bed."

"OK. Call again soon. I love you."

"Love you, too."

CAPE WOOLAMAI WAS my destination today. I had spent a lot of time surfing on the western side of the state. It was time to give the eastern side a try. Statistically speaking, the eastern side had more than half of the top ten surf spots.

Making my way onto the beach, I checked out the waves: one and a half meters. My heart lifted. It was going to be a good day for surfing. I studied the waves to see when and where they were breaking. They were perfect, breaking in the center so I could ride the left or right shoulder.

I paddled out to the line-up, duck diving under the crashing waves along the way. I sat on my board, letting the salt air invade my senses. I took a deep breath in, restoring my inner peace, while my board rose and fell with the swell beneath it. I studied the break and where the good waves were coming from, watching as other surfers took off.

Looking at a guy about six feet away, I called out, "Are there any spots I need to stay clear of?"

"There's a few good rips, but you'll see them easy enough. Apart from that, you should be right."

I nodded my thanks before he took off.

I turned my board to the incoming waves, waiting for the perfect set. As soon as I saw it, I paddled hard. I stayed ahead of it with enough time to compose myself.

Popping up, my feet settled firmly on the board. My stomach lurched as the momentum of the wave spurred me on. I took the right shoulder and rode the wave in. Exhilaration soared through my body, mixed with a sense of being. I was lost in that moment, becoming one with Mother Nature. All other thoughts left my mind.

The wave petered out, and I paddled back to the line-up. Sitting, watching, waiting. The constant breeze in my ears and the sound of waves breaking relaxed me. Lulled by the gentle rise and fall of the swells, I thought about Evie.

She was one of the most complicated people I'd ever met. Whatever she had been through had made her strong and independent. But underneath, she was all doubt. I could see her trying to be brave, but that could change in an instant as her insecurities took over. I felt like it was a fight between Nick and me, and I didn't even know the guy. I didn't know how to beat a ghost. But I would. I would figure it out, and I would gain Evie's trust, bit by bit.

Her. Me. That's what I would strive for.

I STOPPED in at the cat refuge to see how the plans for the reading nook were going. Clarissa and Marjorie had hired a local contractor. His children attended the local primary school, and he had offered to charge the rescue cost-price only. The drawings of the plans were displayed in the foyer for everyone to see. It would be amazing when it was finished.

I was happy to contribute to such a worthwhile project. I enjoyed the anonymous aspect of it, how I got to see and feel their joy firsthand. It was not just a show for me.

Marjorie showed me every last bit of the design, explaining how the cats could also enjoy the area when they were not being read to. They had couches to sleep on and large windows to sun themselves in. The windows had louvres which could be opened in summer to catch the breeze.

There would be an atrium with cat-friendly plants that would be watered automatically using rainwater captured in a tank. The natural light would have a calming effect on the cats, and the ability for them to be able to enjoy direct sunlight and fresh air would be healing.

After discussing all the pros and cons, I went to Mike's enclosure to pay him a quick visit. He did not hear me enter, but as soon as I touched his head, he opened his eyes and regarded me. His purr was almost instant, as was the calming effect he had on me. I couldn't believe I had missed out on the companionship of a pet all my life. Someone who I could confide in and would keep my secrets close.

"How's it going, Mike?"

He head-bumped my hand, a sign to tell me he was good.

"I was thinking about Evie today."

He looked at me as if encouraging me to go on.

"She's pretty special, isn't she?"

He continued giving me that speculative look.

"I like her."

Still, he just stared at me, like I was telling him nothing new.

"Is it that obvious?"

He rolled onto his back, exposing his stomach. I laughed at his pointed reaction.

"Fine, then. It's that obvious. Well, I want you to be the first to know that I am going to do whatever it takes to win her over."

He purred as I stood there, patting him. Such a wise old soul. He would make a family very happy one day.

CHAPTER ELEVEN

EVIE

"STRUTH, Miranda, you didn't say Jesse was such a spunk," Miranda's mum said when Jesse was introduced. She wasn't wrong. Every time I'd looked at Jesse over the past two weeks, I swore he got hotter. I had to remind myself not to stare half the time.

Jesse was going red beside me.

"Spunk means good looking," I whispered to Jesse.

"Nice to meet you, Mrs. Petersen," he said, still blushing.

"We'll have none of that. You call me Jane."

"OK, Jane," Jesse said, giving her a relaxed smile.

"How long are you in Australia for?"

Jesse glanced sideways at me before answering. I tugged at the hem of my t-shirt, looking anywhere but at him.

"I'm not sure," he said. "I've extended my visa to twelve months."

Lightness filled my body as my heartbeat slowed at his words. He took hold of my hand. Electricity shot through my arm, and then my heartrate increased twofold. My poor heart. Slow, fast, slow. It was as confused as my brain.

"Take your bags inside. We've set up mattresses in the lounge room."

"Thanks, Jane," I said, kissing her on the cheek. Jane was everything a mum should be—loving, protective, generous. Sometimes I envied the twins. My own mother couldn't hold a candle to her. And my dad was nothing like Brad, who was jovial, interested in all his children, and supportive. I didn't miss my parents. But I did miss what they should have been.

Lunch was laid out for us on the patio. It was like a party on steroids, and I'm sure Jane laid on the Australian theme just for Jesse. There were musk sticks in jars, peppermint crisps, Tim Tams, lamingtons, Anzac biscuits, pumpkin scones, Milo, pavlova, Twisties, party pies, and sausage rolls. I explained it all, and Jesse took it all in stride until his eyes fell on the fairy bread.

"What is that?"

"Fairy bread. A party is not a party without fairy bread: white bread and butter, covered in hundreds and thousands, always cut into triangles."

"Hundreds and thousands?"

I rolled my eyes. "Coloured sprinkles."

"And you feed this to children?"

"Ah, yeah."

His only response was to shake his head.

"We have hundreds of animals that can kill you, and you're worried about kids eating fairy bread?"

He had a lot to learn if he thought loading your child up on bread and sugar was a problem. It surprised me. From what I knew, Americans loved their sugar.

"What do you want to try first?"

"What's your favourite?"

"Probably party pies and sausage rolls with some dead horse."

His head whipped around with wide eyes, and I giggled.

"Dead horse is tomato sauce. It rhymes."

"Right."

I placed a couple of each on his plate with some tomato sauce on the side and watched while he took his first mouthful of a sausage roll. He closed his eyes, and I imagined the meat and mixtures of flavours tantalising his taste buds while the pastry melted in his mouth. Eagerly, I waited for his conclusion. Opening his eyes, he smiled and nodded in appreciation. Two Aussie foods that he could now claim he liked, Aussie pizza and sausage rolls. I had to admit, he had good taste.

"LET'S GO FOR A SWIM," Miranda said after lunch, grabbing a pile of towels Jane had ready for us.

I didn't follow. I don't know why I felt nervous. I'd spent two years learning to love my body again. To learn to love the curves that made me, me. I wasn't fat, but I wasn't tall and slender like Georgia, or a little pocket-rocket full of muscle like Miranda. When you've been hated on for so long, you end up hating yourself too. I didn't anymore, but the thought of exposing myself like that to Jesse made my stomach clench. I don't know why. He always said nice things about my body.

"Evie, are you coming?" Georgia asked as she headed towards the pool.

"Yeah, I'll be there in a minute," I said, heading into the loungeroom.

When I was alone, I sat heavily on the couch. I tried to hold back my tears. I was angry at myself for overthinking it. I should have just gone with them. If I went out now, I would draw more attention to myself. Then I would feel more self-conscious. I got angrier for feeling self-conscious in the first place and caring about what anyone thought.

The problem wasn't just that I was worried about exposing my body. It was also about exposing my heart. Tears flowed freely — tears of anger, fear, and frustration.

"Evie," Jane called my name as she entered.

I looked at her, trying to smile while I wiped at my tears.

"Evie, honey, what's wrong?" she asked, sitting beside me and pulling me close. The kindness in her voice set my tears flowing again.

"Nothing," I said, my voice breaking.

"OK, we'll sit here until nothing goes away, shall we?"

"Is Jesse OK?"

"He's having a chat with Nana. He's very nice, taking the time to stop to talk to her."

I nodded. Jesse was always very nice. Why would anyone that nice be interested in me? And why did I care, anyway? I didn't want a boyfriend. I was better off alone. Why did I think getting close to him was OK? The despair built up in me again, clutching at my throat. Jane held me while I cried.

The door opened, and footsteps come our way.

"Evie?" Jesse asked.

Jane turned towards him. "Jesse, sweetie, we'll be out in a minute, OK?"

"OK." He didn't leave straight away. I could see him from his knees down, and his feet stood firm. After a moment, he turned and left.

I tried to get my crying under control; my deep breaths were half sobs.

"That man likes you a lot."

I nodded.

"Are you scared?"

"Yes," I whispered. Saying it out loud was as scary as the feeling itself. I was sure she would be able to hear the thumping of my heart and the anguish tearing at my soul.

"Miranda and Jonas think he is wonderful. They're smart; they would see straight through any bullshit."

"He is wonderful."

"I know it's hard to trust again when you've been hurt so badly. But you need to try. Otherwise, you will miss out on many of life's joys."

I nodded. My breathing was coming easier now. What she said was true. I needed to take baby steps, and so far, Jesse had respected that. He never pushed me. He never pushed himself onto me.

I wiped my eyes as Jane gave me a final squeeze.

As we walked outside, I saw Jesse walking off with Nana. She was holding onto his arm, smiling up at him while he spoke.

I smiled.

Brad came and stood beside us. "I haven't seen Nan this happy in a long time. Her laughter is like the sweet chime of bells."

He put his arm around Jane, and they smiled at each other.

"Jesse said he will meet you at the pool," Brad said. "You'd better be careful, Evie. You might need to keep him away from Nan, or she might just steal your man."

After all my avoidance, I was relieved and excited when

Jesse came to join us in the pool. As he pulled his t-shirt off, I marvelled at his toned, tanned body. He may not have a six-pack, but he didn't need it with that magical v line.

"Holy smokes. He is hot," Miranda said, sidling up to me.

I couldn't manage to say a word. I blushed furiously instead.

"No budgie smugglers, Jesse?" Jonas called out.

"I didn't want to embarrass you with my manhood," Jesse quipped.

"He doesn't need budgie smugglers to achieve that," Georgia said to Miranda and me, her eyes wide. "How does someone get a body like that?"

"He surfs and runs. Pretty sure he lifts weights too," I replied. I watched him as he hopped into the water and made his way over to me.

"You better be careful when he does you. Imagine the size of the other muscle," Miranda said, giggling as she and Georgia swam away.

My blush deepened so much my face burned.

"You stay away from my nana with a body like that. She might have a heart attack," Jonas joked.

Nan called out in her raspy voice, "I'll let you know your pop looked like that in his younger years. It helped him snag a good sort like me. The sex was good too. Seven children proved that."

"Nan," multiple voices exclaimed at once.

"Jonas, maybe you should start looking after yourself better," Brad called out. "We need a good daughter-in-law like Evie."

"I don't think it will happen, especially with your genes running through my body, Dad."

Miranda laughed heartily. "Burn."

Jesse took his place by my side and put his arm around my shoulders.

"Feeling better?" he asked, giving my shoulder a squeeze.

CHAPTER TWELVE

JESSE

"YES. SORRY ABOUT LEAVING YOU ALONE," Evie said, looking at me.

"Nana and I had a grand old time. Anything you want to talk about?"

"Not yet."

She gave me a small smile before looking away. I felt encouraged. She hadn't shut me down completely.

I looked at her full lips, thinking how they would feel on mine, imagining how soft and luscious they would be. I wanted to hold her close and be lost in our kiss. My heart beat faster, thinking about it. The throb went all the way down to my crotch. I forced myself to look away. It wasn't the right time. She had been crying only a few minutes earlier.

Nan had told me it wasn't because of me.

"Evie's crying," I'd said to Nan on our walk.

"It's not because of you, dear. Evie's fighting with herself—her fear. The fight will be over soon."

"Is this because of Nick? What did he do to her?"

"I don't know, Jesse. No one knows."

"Even after two years, she hasn't told any of you?"

"No. I think she just wants to forget. The fear has built a wall around her heart." She became silent for a minute as we'd continued our walk. "I am old and wise, and I can tell you one thing for sure, Evie will find her way to you soon."

"I hope so."

"You are the first person in two years she has even taken a second look at."

I'd nodded. There'd been nothing else to say. There was nothing else to do but wait, even if it killed me.

Evie and I watched as Miranda and Jonas set a net up across the pool. The others chatted in excitement, deciding who would be on what team for water volleyball. It surprised me when they split Evie and me up.

"Ready?" Evie asked, pushing off the wall and rising out of the water, facing me. Droplets of water glistened on her olive skin. My eyes were drawn to a drop rolling down her chest between her breasts. I couldn't take my eyes away even after it disappeared. I should have. I was rock hard in my shorts, and staring at her breasts was not helping my situation.

"Stop consorting with the enemy and get over here," Jonas called out to me.

I drew my eyes away, relieved at the distraction.

The twins played hard, and they played to win. They would use any tactic in their toolbox. If a ball was high, Jonas would pick Miranda up so she could pelt it back. They would call out to the other team, especially Evie, and say something about me to distract her.

"Hey, Evie, are you gonna practice making seven babies tonight?" Miranda called out right before she hit the ball in

Evie's direction. Evie was so busy not knowing where to look, she missed the ball even though it was an easy shot.

"Evie, don't listen to them," Georgia said.

Evie set her jaw and turned to face us.

"Better be careful, she's gonna crack a darkie," Jonas teased in a singsong voice.

"Shut up and play the game," Georgia called out.

Out of nowhere, someone made a running jump into the pool. Water splashed everywhere. What emerged was a guy built like a tank. He grabbed Evie and Georgia by the waists and pulled them toward him, planting a huge kiss on each of their cheeks.

"My favorite girls," he exclaimed.

"Lachie, let us go," Georgia said, laughing.

"No way. It's rare that I get to see such beauties out here," he said before kissing them both again.

I didn't know who he was, but I would have preferred if he let go of Evie. I didn't like the way he was holding her so close. Or the way she seemed comfortable with it.

"Lachie, let us go," Evie said, squirming and laughing.

"I'll let you go if you give me a kiss."

I grunted unintentionally. In slow motion, his eyes came to land on me. He looked me up and down. His muscles flexed as he held the girls tighter.

"Who's the underwear model?"

"That's Evie's boyfriend," Georgia said.

I liked the sound of that. What I didn't like was the grin that spread across his face. He whispered something to Evie, and she giggled. Usually, I found the sound pleasant, but right then, it created a hot flash in my vision.

"Who's winning the game?"

He still held onto the girls. Still.

"We are, by three points. Off you go," Miranda said.

"I think I'll stay over here, thanks. I know your dirty tactics. I need to give these girls a fighting chance."

I wasn't pleased about that. Or about the way Evie didn't move away from him. He called them all into a huddle to talk tactics, I presumed. Evie shook her head while everyone else nodded at her.

"You lot having a CWA meeting?" Miranda called out.

They split apart then — Evie and Lachie, the tank, standing side by side, almost touching. My muscles tightened. Lachie served the ball right to me, but I couldn't move fast enough. It landed in the water. He whispered something to Evie, making her roll her eyes. I clenched my teeth. He served the ball to me again, but this time Jonas intercepted and sent the ball flying back. Lachie grabbed Evie by the waist, lifted her up, and she sent the ball soaring my way. I was at least able to hit it this time, and Jonas got the rebound. The whole time I could not take my eyes off them. We missed the return ball.

They gave each other a round of high fives. Lachie served again. Again, I missed the ball. He picked up Evie and spun her around before planting a kiss on her cheek. If I had clenched my jaw any tighter, it might have dislocated.

"Come off it, Lachie. Stop making Jesse jealous."

"What are you talking about?" he protested. "Evie promised herself to me first."

"Seriously, Lachie, we all know you're gay," Miranda yelled at him.

My head snapped toward Miranda. Gay? Shaking my head, I closed my eyes and took a deep breath. When I opened them, Lachie was making his way toward me. He clapped me on the shoulder.

"Sorry, mate, all's fair in love and war, or in this case, volleyball."

"No problem," I said, smiling at him as relief coursed through my body.

Miranda and Jonas were pissed. They both stood with their arms crossed, throwing dirty looks at their brother.

"Don't crack a wobbly. You always play dirty," he said.

He grabbed Jonas in a headlock and rubbed his knuckles into his skull.

Evie came over and smiled apologetically.

"You should be sorry," I said.

I wrapped my arm around her waist, pulling her toward me and kissing her gently on the lips. It may have only been a peck, but as her soft lips touched mine, desire curled through my veins—all of my veins. My erection was instant again. I held her close, skin against skin. I looked into her eyes, completely under their spell. Her hands made their way to my chest, and she gently pushed herself away.

I was lucky I wasn't wearing budgie smugglers, or the whole world would have seen my need for her.

———

WE SAT around the bonfire watching Lachie and Jonas as they opened their bottle of beer and raced each other to finish it in a skulling contest. Evie and I sat next to each other on a log, holding hands. Jonas won by a fraction of a second. He did a victory dance around the fire, high-fiving everyone as he passed.

"What's your talent, Jesse?" Lachie asked. "Being an underwear model doesn't count."

I shifted uncomfortably. This was an area of conversation I always tried to avoid.

"He has an extraordinary talent," Evie said.

As the hair on the back of my neck lifted, the rest of my

body froze. I didn't know what to say. I didn't want to tell them about my memory. I remembered when Granma was looking after me once, and she encouraged me to go to a high school party. Everyone had a few drinks. Two jocks started peppering me with questions about football statistics, getting great joy when I answered them all right. A crowd had formed around us, and everyone started throwing questions at me. They made a game out of it, circling me, hurtling questions at me as fast as I could answer them. If I answered a question right, the inquirer had to have a shot. Soon everyone was tanked, except for me. I hated being the center of attention. I just wanted to be able to enjoy the party like everyone else. As the alcohol started to numb their minds, I escaped. That was the last high school party I went to. I thought then that what my mother had been telling me for years was true. People didn't actually like me. They liked my abilities.

I turned to Evie, shocked she would bring it up. She had never betrayed my confidence before.

"Oh, I'm sure he has," Miranda said, smirking.

"For goodness' sake, keep your mind out of the gutter," Evie said.

Everyone laughed. Except for me.

"I was talking about his superhero impersonation."

"You call hitting the ground at great velocity a talent?" Jonas asked.

I let out a breath and clutched Evie's hand tighter.

"How about you give us a demonstration?" Lachie asked.

"It's reserved for special people," I said.

"What—we aren't special enough?"

"He means special, you know, special with girl parts," Miranda said.

"Not just any girl with girl parts though. Just Evie and her girl parts," Georgia said, laughing.

Evie blushed deeply and mumbled, "Shut up."

Jonas put an arm around her shoulders. Laughing, he said, "Taking the piss out of you is so easy, and you reward us every time."

CHAPTER THIRTEEN

EVIE

I PLAYED the phone call with Shane over in my mind again. I needed to put my wariness aside. I needed to try to open myself up more.

As our line moved towards the doors of the nightclub, Jesse rested his hand on the small of my back. I could feel it distinctly through my short, sequined dress. Tingles radiated from the spot where his hand rested. I didn't flinch away from his touch. I welcomed it. After spending nearly every day with him over the past few months, I didn't find him threatening in the slightest. My heart told me I could trust him, but my mind, and fear, constantly fought with it.

"You look beautiful," he said, out of nowhere.

"Thank you. Do you enjoy dancing?" I asked.

"I wouldn't say it's something I often do," he said, looking down at his feet.

"Don't worry. If you're anything like Jonas, after a couple of drinks, you'll think you're a dance star."

I don't know if my laughter was reassuring or not.

"Hey, I heard that," Jonas said indignantly.

"Just stating facts. You're a two-pot screamer."

"Am not."

As soon as we got in, we headed straight to the bar for a couple rounds of shots. The liquid burned on the way down and lit me up from the inside. I was pumped and ready to dance. Grabbing the girls' hands, I led them out onto the dancefloor. Dancing gave me a sense of freedom I rarely felt. It was like new life flowing through my veins.

I kept our circle small, ignoring any males trying to join us. I wasn't there for them. I was there to enjoy myself. I let the music move me. It pulsed in the hand I had thrown in the air, breaking through my fingertips, travelling through my veins like rhythmic electricity.

There was a break in the set as they swapped DJs, and we headed back to the table. The boys had a drink and some water waiting for us. I downed mine in two gulps and headed to the bar. Standing in line, I could feel the guy beside me leering at me. His eyes kept roving over my body. When I glowered at him, he gave me a wink. Ignoring him, I turned my attention back to the line and the bar. I don't know why guys like that would think a girl would be interested in them and their sleaziness. Next thing I knew, his hand was moving on my arse. I glared at him.

"Do you mind?"

"What?" he asked, squeezing.

"Get your hand off my arse."

His hand stayed put. I angled my body away so I could grab his hand. I placed it on his crotch. Guys like this didn't scare me. I had been through real horror. This guy was a peacock, strutting his stuff, not a deadly cassowary. We were in a crowded place. Real horrors, I knew, happened behind closed doors or secluded areas.

"You've got tickets on yourself if you think anyone

would be interested in you." I gave his hand a push. "This is the only action you'll be getting tonight."

"Oh, come on," he said, reaching out and pulling me towards him.

His hand drifted down as he pressed himself into me. I was about to shove him away when his hand suddenly drew away. Once he was detached from me, I took a step away, and Jesse took my place.

"I believe she asked you to leave her alone," Jesse said.

"What's it to you?"

Jesse put his arm around me. "Seeing she's here with me, I'd say a lot."

"Fuck off."

The guy came towards Jesse with his shoulders squared, chest out, and hands fisted. Jesse held his hand out to stop the arse-grabber from getting closer.

"Don't be stupid," Jesse said calmly.

The guy mumbled under his breath and went to throw a punch. Jesse blocked it. He grabbed the guy's arm and said, "I suggest you walk away."

To my surprise, he did, grunting and shoving people aside as he passed.

I gave Jesse a kiss on the cheek. I had never seen anything like that before. He stayed calm and responded without aggression. It was the same temperament he'd always shown.

"Thank you."

"Not a problem," he said, looking down at me. My whole body was drawn to him. It would have been easy for me, right then, to tilt my head up towards his, wrap my arms around him, and kiss him. I imagined his lips on mine, soft, eager. I turned my face to the bar.

Jesse and Jonas joined us on the dancefloor for the next

set. Some guy was watching us, and I gave him a smile. He took that as an invitation to come over and join us. Next thing I knew, he was grinding up against me. For God's sake, all I did was smile at him, just like I smiled at everyone. I looked at Jesse and rolled my eyes. He laughed in return, and I echoed his laughter. Next thing I knew, the guy was curling my long brown hair in his fingers. I tried to pull away as my laughter died in my throat. Jesse's expression became serious as he took a step towards us.

Before I had a chance to say anything, Georgia sidled up to the grinder and said, "Her boyfriend is over there."

The grinding stopped instantly. He looked at Jesse and apologised before disappearing. I don't know why he was apologising to Jesse; it was me he was grinding on. Georgia was so busy laughing at me; all I could do was roll my eyes.

Jesse smiled as he made his way over to me.

"I'll have to keep you under lock and key at this rate. You are too hot for your own good."

He placed his hands on my hips and drew me towards him. Bending his head to mine, he kissed me.

And I let him.

I let him kiss me there, in the middle of the dance floor, with our friends gaping and smiling, and everyone else dancing around us. His lips parted mine gently, and his tongue searched out mine as he held me closer. There was an underlying sweetness mixed with the sharpness of vodka. His earthy scent warmed me. He was tantalising. Everything disappeared except the smell of him and the taste of him. The only thing that didn't disappear was the aching I felt for him.

I DIDN'T KNOW what I'd done. I didn't kiss Jesse just once last night. There were two other passionate kisses. The alcohol had gone to my head, and I'd let my defences down. His charm, compliments, and self-assuredness disarmed me. The comment about him keeping me under lock and key may have sounded good natured and flirty at the time, but now it resounded as a warning in my head.

As I thought about having to face him in a few minutes at the cat rescue, I started to regret it. While I waited for him to arrive, I stood there, with my arms crossed, hugging myself. Within a minute, the quietness had gotten to me, and I started cleaning. I couldn't stay still when I was nervous.

What was wrong with me? One minute I wanted to be with him, and the next, I flung up barriers as quickly as a security screen in a bank under attack.

I couldn't tell Jesse it was wrong to kiss him. I didn't want to hurt his feelings. And it certainly hadn't felt wrong at the time. I knew what the real problem was, and it had nothing to do with Jesse. The problem was all me. Just me. Well, no. Just me and Nick. Not even Nick, but the memory of what he'd done to me and how that made me feel. I never wanted to feel that powerless again. And kissing Jesse opened me up to that.

And then there was the fact that I didn't really know much about him. I thought I knew what type of person he was. He was kind and thoughtful. His actions and words never contradicted that. But I didn't know who he was. Or why he was here. Or how long he would be here for.

I know learning about someone new was part of the adventure. But secrets scared me. Getting close to someone scared me.

"Good morning," Jesse said cheerfully as he joined me

in the enclosure. I glanced at him as he handed me a bottle of water. "I thought you might need this."

"Thanks." I took the bottle, still not looking at him.

Jesse started working beside me, sharing the load, chatting away. "I thought I'd do a marketing campaign for Mike. I'd like to find him a home."

"That's a good idea."

"I've investigated some options. Facebook looks like a good way to go. What do you think?"

"I used Facebook when I first started my business, and it helped me get exposure."

"Excellent. I think some stories in the paper would also be good. It would be great if we could get him and the rescue on some news programs. Lift the profile a little. It might help with donations and volunteers."

"You should go talk with Clarissa and Marjorie."

"I'll wait until we're finished. I don't want to leave you with all the work."

"You go. I'll be right."

He turned his face towards mine. I couldn't bring myself to look back. Why did I kiss him? Why did I have to have feelings for him? Why did I have to complicate things?

He glanced back at me as he left, but I ignored him and threw myself into my work. I tried to avoid him for the rest of the morning. When he came back to help, I sent him to one of the other enclosures. I knew I was acting irrationally. Kissing someone didn't mean you were in a committed relationship. It didn't have to mean anything. But the way I was feeling, and the fact I'd started thinking about him when we weren't together, was dangerous.

CHAPTER FOURTEEN

JESSE

CLARISSA AND MARJORIE were excited by my idea. We took some photos of Mike and came up with a compelling and funny story from his point of view. Something to attract the right family for our special boy.

"How's Evie?" Clarissa asked, giving me a smile.

"I don't know. She's shut down."

"What do you mean?"

"We've been spending quite a bit of time together over the past couple of months, between outings and work. We kissed the other night. Today, she's hardly spoken to me."

"Ah."

Clarissa and Marjorie both reminded me of my grandma because I could be open with them, and they wouldn't judge me. Granma was the only person who always wanted me just to be me. She had wished nothing but happiness for me. When she died, it left me empty. My confidant was gone.

"I'm sure you've heard about Nick by now," Marjorie said.

"I've heard bits and pieces. But none of that has come from Evie."

"I don't think you'll hear the whole story unless it comes from Evie herself. She hasn't shared it with any of us. I guess she wants to put it all behind her and not dwell on it."

"You're right. She isn't dwelling on it. She's always so happy and full of energy."

"Yes, she is," Clarissa said. "But when you came along, I think some old scars opened."

"I don't understand."

"Maybe her fears became real again. It might scare her to have feelings for you because it means she will need to trust you. When you have been hurt that bad, trust is hard."

"What should I do?"

I liked her and wanted to break down those walls.

"Don't give up on her. She opened the door for you. She will again."

"Just don't push her too hard," Marjorie said.

"GOOD MORNING," I said to Evie as I hopped into her car.

"Hi. I've set up a full day's work for you."

"Excellent."

"You will be working on your own today. You've had enough training now. I'm confident you can handle any situation."

"OK."

My heart dropped. I was hoping to be working side by side with her again. If we were going to be honest, my training had been over months ago, but that hadn't stopped her working with me before. She had rebuilt those walls high. I hoped it wouldn't take as long to break them down again. I was ready to work at it, to show her she could trust me.

"I have uploaded the run sheet to your profile."

"Great. Thanks," I said, not really thankful at all.

I opened the app and read through the jobs.

"I saw your Mike post on Facebook yesterday. It was terrific. It sounded exactly like him," Evie said.

"It's had a lot of likes already and has been shared a hundred times."

"Hopefully, his forever family sees it."

I finished reading and switched the phone off.

"Finished already?"

"I'm a quick reader."

"Another one of your talents?"

"Yes," I said, shifting in my seat. I wasn't ready to tell her everything yet, but how could I expect her to trust me if I didn't share?

"Remember how I said at the cricket match sometimes I just like to be normal? What I can do, my memory and reading, is very rare. It means I have a high IQ, which is also rare. Rare is not normal. Most people who know me don't treat me like I'm normal."

"Just because you have rare talents doesn't mean you're not normal. We all think differently and process things differently. If we are to use your reasoning, that would mean none of us are normal."

"Yes. That's true. My grandma was one of only a few people who treated me the same as everyone else. She kept me grounded. When she died, I couldn't stand to be home anymore. I never felt like I belonged. So, I came here, for a break, and to re-center myself."

This was the first time I had spoken about how I felt

since Granma died. A weight lifted off my chest as I shared it with her. I wanted to share more, to tell her how my family made me feel, but we'd arrived at the apartment building.

"Do you want to meet for lunch? We can go to the café on Smith Street," I said.

"Sounds good." She smiled at me.

I watched her walk away. My eyes stayed glued to her hips.

CLARISSA SPOKE EXCITEDLY through the phone. "Jesse, good news. Your marketing campaign worked. A family wants to adopt Mike."

"That's wonderful."

"They sound ideal. They have two younger kids and a teenager."

"He'll love that. He loves kids."

"They live in Perth. Marjorie and I wondered if you would travel over with him to get some promo shots. It'll round off the story beautifully."

"Sure. When do you need me to go?"

"Saturday would be ideal."

"I'll need to speak to Evie."

"It's OK. We've already spoken to her. She can fill your shifts if you want to spend some time over there."

"OK. Great." Although, I wasn't sure if it was great. I didn't want to spend time away from her and risk losing what we had built. Not that I knew what we had built exactly. Ever since the kiss, she was standoffish.

"We'll email your ticket to you. Be at the airport at nine."

I was happy for Mike. I hoped he was going to his perfect forever home. The beautiful boy deserved the best.

CHAPTER FIFTEEN

EVIE

"EVIE, WHAT ARE YOU DOING HERE?' a voice I recognised asked.

I looked up at Jesse, who was staring down at me in the boarding lounge at the airport.

"I'm going to Perth with Mike. What are you doing here?"

"I'm going to Perth with Mike?" he said, cocking his head.

I think it dawned on us at the same time.

"Clarissa," we said in unison.

I rang the rescue as I walked to a secluded corner. Jesse followed me. I put the phone on speaker.

"Marjorie," I said when she answered.

"Evie, is everything OK?" she asked, concerned.

"Where's Clarissa?"

"I'll go get her. Is everything OK? Why are you calling?"

I didn't answer her as we waited for Clarissa to join her on the phone.

"Hello, Evie. I assume Jesse is there with you, and that's why you're calling?"

Marjorie gasped. "Clarissa, what have you done?"

"I did nothing a wise old woman wouldn't. I arranged for a hard-working woman to have a two-week holiday. And I'm hoping she'll take Jesse with her."

I said nothing. What was there to say? Minutes ago, I was thinking about how much I would miss Jesse as I made my two-week road trip back home. And now, if he accepted Clarissa's proposition, I would spend every minute with him.

Jesse was silent beside me as he stared at the phone.

"You're welcome, dear," Clarissa said before hanging up.

Jesse raised his gaze from the phone to my face. He didn't say anything. His eye contact was unwavering, and he expelled a long breath. I felt myself breaking into a sweat as my heart rate doubled.

"You ready for a road trip?" I asked hesitantly.

"Yes," he said, a huge smile lighting his face.

"I'M SORRY, love. All our campervans are out on hire. The only thing I can give you is a bigger van. But it's still only a two berth," the booking agent said to me as her eyes drifted over to Jesse. I felt my jaw tense as she gave him a slow smile.

Right, so we'd have to share a bed. We were both adults. I'm sure we could handle sleeping in the same bed. And the van was made for two people. Surely, there would be enough room to live comfortably. I looked at Jesse.

"OK. We'll take the bigger van, thanks," I said, drawing her attention back to me.

"Who will be driving?" she asked, gazing at Jesse.

"We will both be driving," he said.

I instinctively moved closer to him, uncomfortable with the way she kept ogling him.

We finished the paperwork and were introduced to our home for the next two weeks. The white van had sleek lines. The inside was fresh and clean, with plenty of storage. The cupboards were a light brown woodgrain making the interior feel fresh and airy. It had everything we needed including a toilet and shower. I thought about being that close to Jesse, naked. My stomach clenched. And then I thought about him being naked, less than a metre away from me in the shower. His tanned, muscled body glistening with water. I bit my bottom lip and blushed profusely.

Jesse broke into my thoughts, saying, "Let's go to dinner tonight. I hear the restaurant at Kings Park is beautiful."

"I don't have anything to wear. I only brought casual clothes."

"We can go shopping. We have plenty of time."

It was true. Dropping Mike off had taken hardly any time at all. His new family had been lovely. They had shown us all around their house and introduced us to their cat and dog. The twin eight-year-old girls showed us their bedrooms, where they hoped Mike would sleep. Mike had been so chill when he walked out of his cage. He'd hopped up onto the couch and sat between the girls, happily receiving their pats. Jesse took a few photos to share on Facebook.

Getting dressed in close proximity to each other was difficult. As I bent down to take my shorts off, I hoped Jesse wasn't doing the same because a bum bump would be embarrassing. Just as embarrassing as him sneaking a look at the wrong time. And then my mind drifted again, thinking about how close he was to me, and my heart raced. Seriously, I needed to control this shit.

I turned to face Jesse. The navy shirt he was wearing intensified his blue eyes. I noticed the way his shoulders tapered down to his waist. His hips. For God's sake, lift your eyes, I told myself. When I looked up, Jesse was staring at me, his eyes lingering on my boobs, which now felt exposed in the low-cut V-neck dress.

"You look beautiful," he said, while I stood there blushing.

"Thank you. You look quite nice yourself."

"I bought you something."

He handed me a padded box. His hand was shaking as I took it from him. Inside, on a gold chain, sat a beautiful heart pendant with a single diamond. I gasped. It made me feel nervous, receiving something so beautiful from him. I hesitated before leaning towards him, giving him a kiss on the cheek.

"Thank you, Jesse."

———

FRASERS RESTAURANT WAS EXQUISITE. Its curved structure and floor-to-ceiling windows took advantage of the amazing view. It overlooked the perfectly manicured gardens of Kings Park. In the last of the daylight, we could see sailboats anchored on the river below. The city lights sparkled in the distance.

"Do you have a reservation, sir?" the waitress asked.

"No, sorry. It was a last-minute decision."

"Are you celebrating a special occasion?"

"Yes, it's our first date."

"I will speak to the maître d' to find you the perfect table."

Is that what this was? A first date? The stakes felt higher, and my nerves intensified. She led us to a table by the window, Jesse guiding me with his hand on my back. It felt strong, warm and comforting.

"The maître d' has gifted you a glass of champagne for this momentous occasion. I will be back shortly to take your drink order."

"What type of wine would you like?" Jesse asked, handing me the menu.

"You choose, as long as it's not red. Red gives me a headache."

"We will have a bottle of the Massolino Moscato, please," Jesse said when the waitress returned.

"Nice choice, sir. I am sure the lady will appreciate its seductive flavour."

I stared at the menu in wonder. How was I ever going to choose? I scanned through the choices and the prices and thought, 'We're not in Kansas anymore, Toto.'

"Any thoughts?" Jesse asked.

"Uh, no. What about you?"

"Would you like to start with some oysters?"

"OK."

"How many would you like? Six?"

"Yes, please."

After we made our dinner choices, we sat there in silence. I didn't know what to say. I didn't know where to look. I looked at Jesse. I looked down at the table. Out the window. I felt my heart beating hard in my chest and was surprised it couldn't be heard in the silence between us.

"Evie, what's wrong?"

I didn't even know how to answer. I raised the glass of wine to my lips and took a gulp. I didn't even taste the wine. If I didn't say something soon, I might actually start crying from all the pent-up emotions. I started tapping my knife on the table. Jesse reached over and took hold of my hand. His touch was reassuring. I lifted my eyes to his.

"I'm feeling nervous. It's been a long time since I've been on a date."

"Evie, it's just me. We've spent the last ten hours together. We've spent nearly every day for the last few months together. It's no different because we're at a dinner table."

"True."

I let out a long breath, trying to expel my nerves.

"It's been a long time since I've been on a date where the person wants to spend time with me. Usually, they want something out of me," he said.

I looked at him closely, and he gave me a half smile.

"What do you mean?"

CHAPTER SIXTEEN

JESSE

I WANTED to tell her everything. My memory. My skills. How they could be exploited. My money. That the money was what people cared about. Not me. Just my money. My billions of dollars. Even my family were just interested in the money. But I didn't want to risk her seeing me differently. What if she just thought of me as a gravy train?

I tried to tell myself my fears were unreasonable. She was successful in her own right. She was happy within herself. What I could add to her life would only complement her.

But I couldn't. I couldn't tell her all of it.

I settled on part of it.

"People see me as something they can use to make money or make themselves look good. They like to take me gambling so I can count cards. Or they like to make bets with people about how much I can remember. They use my mind to find out what the best investments are or what horses are likely to win races. They want to be my friend because they can get something out of it. Or they want to date me because it makes them look good or stand out."

"That must be a lonely life."

Our entrée arrived. It sat between us untouched.

"It is. Even as a child, my parents would enter me into competitions for their own benefit. My grandma was never like that. When I went to visit her, she would want to talk about me. My dreams. How I would like a family one day. What I wanted my life to look like someday. She never asked me for anything or expected anything."

"How do you trust anyone?" she asked while holding onto her new pendant.

"I don't. I prefer not to tell anyone about what I can do. But word gets around. People find out. I don't have many friends because I don't know who is genuine. But you are different. You have never drawn attention to it. You've kept my secret for me. Thank you."

"If it's any consolation, I am glad you're here. Not your abilities, just you," she said, smiling at me. "Although your mapping skills may come in handy."

The tenseness left me at her words. She knew my memory was like no other. But she didn't continually refer to it or draw any attention to it.

She was still fiddling with the pendant, which drew my eyes to it. And there, as if inviting me to stare at them, were her perfectly rounded breasts. I imagined caressing them, kissing them, and felt an instant stir in my crotch. I tore my eyes away. She was watching me. I felt a hot flush rise in my cheeks. She'd caught me once again.

"So, what do you have planned for the next two weeks?" I asked, trying to take my mind off ravishing her body.

"A few things. But I want you to have some input, too. It's not just about me."

"I'm happy to do what you've planned," I said, thinking about how generous she was even though I had crashed her party. Waiting for an answer, I ate an oyster, relishing in the salty softness of the flesh.

"Jesse, this is your holiday, too. I want to do things you would like to do." Her voice was firm. I was not accustomed to someone being so considerate of me. The girls in my life before just wanted to go where they could be seen and do what would make them look good. They didn't ask me what I wanted to do. Evie popped an oyster in her mouth as if she were emphasizing that she was waiting for me to answer.

"I would like to go surfing in Margaret River. I hear it has some great surf spots and nice swells."

"That could be fun. I've never surfed before. Maybe I can set a new wipe-out record."

"I'm sure you'd be no different to me when I started out."

"We can head there tomorrow and then onto Pemberton. I'd like to climb a fire tree."

"A fire tree?"

"There's a network of eight trees with lookouts at the top of them. They used the lookouts to spot fires before spotter planes were introduced. The only way to spot fires was to be at the top of the canopy. You climb up to the lookouts using metal spikes that spiral the tree. One hundred and sixty-five spikes, to be exact. It's seventy-five meters up to the platform."

The more she spoke, the more my stomach flipped. I was not fond of heights.

"Right, and you want to climb it?"

"Absolutely, imagine the view from up there."

"Do we get harnessed in or anything?"

"No. And there's no net to catch you if you slip. How cool is that?" she asked.

"Your cool and my cool are two entirely different

things," I said. A nervous laugh escaped.

"Don't you like heights?"

Her eyes watched me closely.

"Not particularly. On our bush walk at Werribee Gorge, I made sure I stayed away from the edge of the cliff. Looking down would have scared the bejeezus out of me."

"You don't have to climb if you don't want to. I won't mind."

"Let's see when we get there."

I tried to think brave thoughts.

After dinner, we took a stroll along one of the many pathways. The city lay below us, the lights from the skyscrapers reflected in the Swan River, twinkling like stars. I held Evie's hand; our fingers entwined. As she walked, the slit in her navy dress revealed her tanned leg. It was a stunning dress, revealing much of the body I longed to touch.

Stopping, she turned towards me.

"Thank you for dinner," she said, reaching up to kiss me.

I could feel her breasts pressing against my chest as I held her hips firmly. My hands didn't know which way to go. Towards her curvy butt or her chest. I ran my hands up her ribcage until they settled below her breasts. Just feeling them was enough to make me instantly hard. I was sure she would be able to feel it through my pants. She entwined her arms around my neck and pulled her body closer to mine, deepening the kiss and my urge.

She broke off the kiss, breathing heavily. I rested my forehead against hers, trying to regain composure.

How would I sleep right next to her and not touch her? I wanted to touch her and kiss her every moment of the day. I wished the words 'don't push her too hard' would stop echoing in my ears.

CHAPTER SEVENTEEN

EVIE

LAST TIME I kissed Jesse like that, I had avoided him for days. There was no avoiding him now. We would be spending practically every moment together. I lay beside him in the campervan, listening to his rhythmic breathing. Every time I closed my eyes and thought sleep might envelop my brain, I found my eyes wide open again, without any conscious effort from me. It had been a long time since I'd shared a bed with someone. I usually took up as much of the bed as I liked. Now, every time I moved, I was conscious that I might accidentally touch him.

I needed sleep. Tomorrow was going to be a big day. I listened to his breathing, concentrating only on it, trying to match it. Slowly, I felt myself drifting off.

The sun rose early, filling the van with light and warmth. I would need to remember to draw the curtains from now on. I turned to Jesse, who was already awake, looking at something on his phone. Rubbing the sleep out of my eyes, I sat up next to him.

"Good morning," he said, giving me a smile. "I've been looking into surfing lessons."

"Great. What did you find?"

"The surf school has group lessons and private ones, ranging from beginners to advanced."

"That's good. I could do a group beginner one, and you could do an advanced one?"

"Yeah, that's what I was thinking."

I liked that idea. It would mean he wouldn't be held back by me. He could get out there and enjoy himself on the bigger waves. And being in a group would mean all the attention wouldn't be focused on me.

"It will take us around three hours to get there. Would you like me to make a booking for this afternoon?"

"Yes, please."

"Do you want to shower first?'

"Yeah. OK."

I shimmied my way to the bottom of the bed, conscious of how much I wasn't wearing. I had on PJ shorts and a singlet. I felt exposed, which was silly because he had seen me in shorts and a bikini top, and that dress last night hadn't left much to the imagination.

I didn't look up to see if he was watching me. If he was, I would feel more nervous. I retrieved a towel and some clothes out of my bag. Hugging them to me, I headed straight for the bathroom. It was compact but manageable. Knowing we were using tank water, I showered quickly, choosing not to wash my hair. When I exited the bathroom, Jesse had pulled the bed apart, so we had somewhere to eat breakfast. Fresh air flowed in through the open door.

I prepared breakfast while Jesse showered. Seeing his tanned shoulders and arms exposed when he emerged from the bathroom in a singlet and shorts distracted me. Usually, he wore a t-shirt, and I didn't get to appreciate the sight. I mistimed the toast, and when it popped up, it was a darker shade of brown than intended.

"Smells good," Jesse said. He stepped up behind me and looked over my shoulder. If I moved backwards ever so slightly, I would be able to feel his body heat. I wanted to. I didn't.

"I love the smell of toast, too. There is vegemite on the table for you."

"Ah, vegemite. The thing Australians love and the rest of the world don't understand."

I sat opposite him and watched him butter his toast. He grabbed the jar of vegemite.

"You might want to put it on lightly at first."

He didn't put it on lightly enough. Oh well, it would be his funeral. He handed the jar to me. I laid it back on the table.

"Aren't you having any?'

"No, thanks. I don't like it."

He looked at me with wide eyes, like I was insulting my culture. The fact was I hated the taste. I tried it once and never went back again. When I watched the videos of people tasting it, I could totally relate.

"So, you're not a Happy Little Vegemite?'

"Don't need to eat yeast extract to be happy."

I watched him as he ate. His nose wrinkled as he smelled it. He took a bite and chewed. His whole face twisted as his mouth opened, and he cringed. His face contorted, and he swallowed. He pushed the plate away, shaking his head violently, his mouth open and twisted. I cringed with him.

I was laughing so hard tears rolled down my cheeks.

"What the hell was that? That is not food."

He was still cringing and shaking his head. I handed him a glass of water and my buttered toast.

"Don't be insulting. It's an Australian staple, you know."

"That you don't eat."

"Yeah, well, I'm not stupid."

"I can't even describe it. It is just—oh God, it's just bad."

I was still laughing.

I had videoed the whole thing and couldn't wait to send it to Georgia. I showed him the phone.

"If this ends up on YouTube, I'm not responsible."

He shook his head.

AS WE CHANGED into our wetsuits, I glanced over at Jesse. His tanned body was a sight to behold. He caught me looking, and I turned away, blushing.

"These wetsuits are not easy to get into. It's like getting into skin-tight jeans," I said, as I tried to wriggle my way in.

"It's a skill you learn over time. I would teach you, but after that vegemite stunt this morning, I don't think you deserve my help."

He laughed as I jumped and lifted my wetsuit, so it got past my butt and was loose around my crotch.

"That's not fair. I told you to spread it lightly."

I started working on my arms. When the wetsuit was up over my shoulders, Jesse came over to help zip it up. He was always attentive. He knew when I was feeling sad and would ask if I was OK. He brought me water the morning after the nightclub. He listened to everything I said. If we were meeting a new client or dog, he always let me take the lead, never interrupting or trying to show off. He never let me put myself down. He thanked me for being me. He made me feel good.

The instructor came in and gave us a once-over before giving us a surf school rashie to put over our wetsuit.

"Evie, you can follow Jesse and his instructor to the beach if you like. Your lesson is in an hour. You are the only one booked so far. I'll come and get you when its time."

"OK."

I was excited about being able to watch Jesse surf. He had been out to Torquay and Bells Beach at least once a week since I'd met him. Surfing was a passion for him. Before Jesse and his instructor headed to the water, I gave him a kiss on the cheek and said, "Have fun."

They paddled out and sat on their boards, waiting for a wave. Like fluid motion, they dropped flat and paddled. Then, as if it was no effort at all, they stood up on their boards. Their boards were extensions of their bodies, not inanimate objects they were standing on. I twisted and turned with him, even though I was standing stock still on the sand. The way the board caressed the wave was beautiful. It glided and cut through the water. I held my breath when it looked like he was being consumed by a barrel, relieved when he emerged still upright. Power and balance. Smoothness and precision. Pure elegance.

When it was my turn, I followed the instructor back to the other end of the beach, where the waves were calmer.

"Ok. The first part of the lesson is not actually in the water. You'll learn how to position yourself on the surfboard, how to paddle, and the technique to stand up."

We got the positioning right and then the paddling. How the thumb enters the water first, how to move our arms, so we are pushing and not pulling, always looking forward. Then I started learning how to get up on the board. He showed me first. He made it look easy – lift your chest with your elbows up, get up onto one knee, keeping a ninety-degree angle, swing the other leg forward so your knee is at your chest, lift the knee that is still on the board and stand with both knees bent, keeping most weight on the back foot so the nose of the board stays out of the water.

Easy, right? Maybe if you've done it a hundred times. After a few attempts, I wasn't too bad at it. But how would I manage in the water when the surface below me wasn't hard and unmoving?

We went out into the water and faced the beach. The instructor stood holding the front of the board waiting for the perfect swell, which would form into the perfect wave. When he saw it, he told me to paddle. I wasn't fast enough, and the swell surged underneath me and disappeared.

We tried again, but this time he stood at the back and gave me a little push. I got up onto my knee, and as I swung my leg around, I lost balance and fell off the side. I was laughing so much I continually had to spit saltwater out of my mouth.

We tried again. This time I got to my feet. In my excitement, I looked back at my instructor instead of forwards and fell off. We tried again. And again.

On my final attempt, I made it all the way to the shallows standing on my board. The instructor came running up behind me and wrapped me in a bear hug. I hugged him back. I couldn't stop smiling.

Jesse was watching from the beach. I undid my leg strap and ran to him, dumping the board before I reached him. Grabbing me around the waist, he spun me around before kissing me.

"That was so much fun. Thank you," I said, wrapping my arms around him again.

"You looked great out there."

"Thank you. I loved watching you. You were amazing."

"I got some great tips I can use for years to come. Thank you for coming with me."

CHAPTER EIGHTEEN

JESSE

WE WALKED hand in hand along the 1.8-kilometer-long Busselton Jetty. Working on an average of 0.762 steps per meter, if we walked to the end, it would be 2,362 steps. The aged wood beneath our feet showed what years of being subjected to the elements looked like. Deep set grooves and roughness gave it a rustic beauty. The water below us was a clear azure blue that lapped gently against the wooden piles. The sun was sitting low in the sky, its warmth diminishing by the minute.

Evie stopped walking and stared out across the water before looking down. There were some stairs leading to a landing below. It was deserted with no boats tied up or humans using it for swimming.

"This looks like a nice spot to eat. What do you think?" she said.

"Looks great."

We took the stairs to the lower level and spread the fish and chips out between us. Taking our flip-flops off, we hung our feet over the edge. The sun kissed the horizon, spreading warm golden hues across the water. Looking at

Evie, with her face awash in golden light and the golden tones in her brown hair highlighted, I thought about how perfect the day was.

Evie made everything a delight. She readily laughed, even if it was at herself. I'd watched her during her lesson. Every time she fell off the board, she laughed so heartily the instructor joined in. He didn't have to persuade her to get back on the board. She had done so as soon as she could control her laughter. She tried and tried again, never giving up, no matter how many times she hit the water. Her care-free, happy nature was so infectious people could not help but be drawn to her and like her.

But sometimes, like this moment, when she was deep in thought, her eyes showed something different. Something deep-seated. Her eyes were troubled, but her face so passive it wasn't easily noticeable.

I wanted to know what her conflict was. I wanted to share the pain with her so I could help wash it away. Forever. So, she didn't have to feel it again. But the only way I could do that was if she opened up to me. Sometimes, I thought she might be opening the door, but as soon as she realized it was ajar, she would close it again.

"What are you thinking about?" I asked her.

"About how wonderful the day was." She turned to me and smiled a wistful smile.

"You looked very serious. Like something was troubling you."

"I was thinking about what you said last night, about how people would make you do things for their own benefit. My ex was like that too. Everything was about him. He wouldn't have been happy for me today, like you were, unless he could take credit for it somehow. He wouldn't have finished his lesson and watched me like you did. And if he did, he would have been angry at my laughter and failed attempts."

When she stopped talking, I didn't say anything. I didn't want to stop her flow of words. I knew she didn't open up to people. Her friends all knew bits and pieces, but no one knew the whole truth.

"When you live with someone like that, you lose yourself. You're told and shown over and over again how insignificant you are that you believe it."

Now I didn't talk because I didn't want to interrupt her; I was stunned into silence.

"You are different, Jesse. I don't think you have a selfish or violent bone in your body. I really like you, and it scares me."

I didn't want to tell her I was scared too. This was her moment of honesty. I wanted to let her own it. Even though I knew the next words could sound empty, I meant them. I wanted her to believe me.

"I won't hurt you, Evie. I think you are wonderful. You are smart and kind and funny—not to mention beautiful. Spending time with you is a joy."

───────

"IT'S time to immerse yourself in some Australian culture," Evie said, grabbing her laptop. "There's a whole list of movies you should watch."

"As long as it's nothing like vegemite."

She laughed as she lay down next to me on the bed.

"You choose a genre, and I'll choose a movie."

"This will be interesting. OK, I'll choose comedy."

"Let's start with a classic. It's a bit before our time but still great. *Crocodile Dundee*, the Australian version."

"There was more than one version?"

"Yes, the other version doesn't have all our slang."

"That's no fun."

She snuggled up to me as the movie started. She didn't even make it halfway through before she fell asleep in my arms. I kept watching anyway. It was such a fun movie, and every time I laughed out loud, I hoped I wouldn't wake her. But I needn't have worried; she only stirred and snuggled in deeper.

When the movie finished, I got up and put the laptop away. Calculating the time difference, I decided to call home to see how everything was going. I went outside, so I didn't wake Evie.

"Hello," April's voice came through the phone.

"Hi, April."

"Jesse, how are you? Where are you?" Her happiness was audible.

"I'm good. I'm in Western Australia at the moment. How are you?"

The slightest pause. No one else would have noticed, but I knew April so well, the pause was like a gaping hole. What was worrying her?

"Good. This management gig is hard work. When are you coming home?"

"I don't know. I had a quick look at the figures. They're looking good."

"Yeah. There have been a couple of questionable acquisitions, but overall, I think the right decisions are being made."

"As long as they can justify their reasoning, that's all I ask."

I walked through the caravan park, keeping my voice low. I didn't want to disturb anyone.

"I had to let Luke go. His interests weren't aligned with yours. He made some acquisitions on friends' businesses that didn't fit our investment portfolio. When I questioned him, he became defensive and didn't seem to care it was your money he was wasting."

"You made the right decision. That's why I left the business in your capable hands," I said, trying to reassure her.

"It's not as easy for me. I can't read numbers like you do."

"Don't worry about looking at them in depth. I can do that from here. That's not why you're there. I trust you to make sure everyone is looking after our best interests."

"I know. But it is a lot of responsibility."

"If you ever change your mind, it's OK."

"Seriously, when are you coming home?"

Looking up at the stars, I marveled at how bright they were. I considered the question. Did I want to go back?

"I don't know. Things are good here. I'm happy."

"Have you found yourself?"

I smiled. I had found much more than just myself.

"I'm getting there."

"Have you found someone else? Is that why you sound strange?"

"I think so."

"What does that mean?"

The twinkling stars reminded me of Evie's eyes when she was teasing me.

"I have found someone I like."

"Does she like you?"

"I think so." No, wait, she said she did. I needed to clarify. "Yes, she likes me."

"Does she know? About you? About the money?"

"She doesn't know about the money."

"So, she likes you for you?'

"Yes."

"Good."

It was good. Everything about Evie was good. Even the push and pull created by her fears was good. Every time she came back, she was stronger. We were stronger. Her feelings were more defined—as defined as the constellations up above me.

"Keep up the good work, April. I'll call in a few days."

"OK. Can you call your mom, so she stops bugging me?"

"I will. Thanks for everything, April. I appreciate it."

"I love you, Jesse."

"Love you too, April."

I would call my mom. But not today. I didn't want to ruin a perfectly good day.

I went back inside and hopped into bed beside Evie. As I put my arm around her, I breathed in her aroma. The rose scent from her shampoo filled my senses. I felt her warmth everywhere our bodies touched. I imagined holding her like this forever as I fell asleep.

I STOOD NEXT TO EVIE, my head tilted back so I could see the top of the fire tree.

"We're climbing that?"

'We're not here to fuck spiders."

I looked at her and could see the laughter emerging. Another one of those startling Australian sayings. I could easily use that one.

She grabbed my hand and gave it a squeeze.

"Jesse, you don't have to come with me."

"I want to."

That wasn't entirely true. I didn't want to climb the tree. But I wanted to go with her. I would follow her into the fiery depths of hell. So why not face one of my greatest fears?

She kissed me then, at the base of that three-hundred-and-fifty-year-old tree. There was no other living soul present, except those ageless trees looking down on us. Silence resounded in our ears.

The warmth of her mouth drew me in until all I was aware of was her tongue searching out mine. A fire burned inside me as her hands found their way under my tank top, clutching my back, drawing me closer. My hand entwined in her ponytail as I cupped the back of her head. I instantly became hard as my other hand found her soft skin under her singlet.

She groaned as my hand made its way around her back, pulling her hips to mine. My hardness intensified until I thought I wouldn't be able to take it anymore. I started to pull back. She drew away. I could barely breathe. My skin tingled where we'd touched. The fire inside lingered.

"For luck," she said, breathless, her eyes searching mine.

"If I die now, I'll die a happy man."

Evie and I made our way to the tree. She placed her palm on the trunk and looked up. I stood next to her, thinking how small and insignificant I felt next to the grand old tree. Evie started climbing. If I concentrated on where I was putting my hands and feet and didn't think about the increasing distance between us and the ground, I was OK.

As we circled and circled, I started to see double. It was disorientating. I paused and peered straight ahead to steady myself. We were past the tops of the smaller trees. I looked up as I gripped the steel rod. We were halfway to the first platform. I didn't glance down. Breathing in, I tried to relax my body before I started to climb again.

With every rung we climbed, it became more difficult. Maybe my mind was playing tricks on me, but it felt like the spikes were getting further apart. Maybe it felt that way because my legs were tiring, straining with each step we made. We made it to the first platform, thirty meters above the ground. I held tight to the railing as Evie walked around the platform taking in the sight.

There were trees as far as we could see. The trees stood close together like an army advancing: straight, tall trunks, leaves, and more trunks. Smooth trunks, almost fawn in color, bare of branches until the top third of the tree. Their leaves grew in clumps. They were glossy, dark green on top, lighter underneath. When a breeze moved them, it reminded me of a kaleidoscope.

I looked up to the lookout above us, knowing we were not even halfway up.

"You can wait here for me if you like," Evie said, giving me an out.

"Nope, not giving up now. I could use another good luck kiss, though."

"You can have a congratulatory one when we reach the top," she said, kissing my cheek on the way past.

I watched her as she started the second climb. I appreciated the view but didn't watch it for long as I needed to start climbing. I tried not to look up too often. It worried me that it felt we were getting nowhere quickly. I didn't look down, either. My legs were shaking as we neared the lookout platform. When we climbed the ladder, and my feet landed on the wooden platform, I was ever so grateful to have stopped climbing. Evie waited at the railing for me, taking hold of my hand as soon as I arrived next to her.

Holding my face, she kissed me tenderly, telling me how proud she was of me, between kisses. We turned back to the view in front of us. I had one arm wrapped around Evie's shoulders, while I gripped the railing with the other hand. The foliage from the top of the magical karri trees stretched all the way to the horizon. Only a handful of trees were higher than we were. It reminded me of an endless green ocean, and those trees that sprouted higher were crests of waves.

I looked down. A sudden wave of dizziness hit me. I gripped the handrail tight. I closed my eyes as Evie's arm tightened around my waist. The firmness of her touch was reassuring. I felt myself swaying. I broke into a cold sweat. I tried to control my breathing, keeping my eyes closed. Evie continued to hold me. If not for her comforting touch, I would have dropped to my knees.

I opened my eyes slowly, making sure I was looking over the treetops. I didn't look down at the ground. Evie was watching me. She reached up with her free hand and cupped the side of my face, keeping eye contact with me.

CHAPTER NINETEEN

EVIE

"ARE YOU OK?" I asked Jesse.

The tendons in his neck were standing out, and his breathing was haphazard. I ran my thumb over his cheek, hoping it would be comforting.

"I...shouldn't...have...looked down."

"Probably not. But braveness is often mixed with a bit of craziness."

"I don't know how I'm going to get down."

"The same way we got up. One step at a time."

He closed his eyes again.

"It's so far down."

"It's 165 steps. As soon as we take the first one, it will be 164. I will be with you the whole way."

Opening his eyes, he took a deep breath in. Sharing someone's fear with them is totally humbling. You feel something for them at that moment that can never be changed. My heart opened to him. I wanted to comfort him, not only because it was the right thing to do, but because I wanted to strengthen him.

"Thank you, Evie."

I suggested I go first, so if I saw Jesse faltering, I could talk him through it. As we descended, I tried to keep him focused by reminding him now and then to relax and breathe. I was scared he would freeze and wouldn't be able to keep moving. When we got to the first platform, I sighed in relief. I waited for Jesse to set his feet down before approaching him.

Wrapping my arms around him, I said, "Not much farther now. You can do this."

I felt his head nod against mine.

When we made it to the bottom, I breathed a deep sigh of relief. The tenseness in my body surprised me. As soon as Jesse's feet hit the ground, I went to him. His breathing was shaky. He hugged me so tightly I feared he might expel the air out of me. When he released me, I looked up at him. His eyes were filled with tears.

"It's OK, Jesse. You're safe now."

"I've never experienced anything like that before. If you weren't there, I would have crumpled to my knees and not moved."

"You were brave. I'm proud of you."

"I think we need to stay away from heights for a while."

"I think we can manage that," I said, giving him a squeeze. "We'll give Valley of the Giants a miss and head straight for Albany."

"What's in Albany?"

"Ghosts."

"Interesting."

"Only if you're lucky."

"I'm feeling pretty lucky. I just defied death."

"I'M VOTING it's a man's job," I said as we both stood looking between the dump point and the waste box on the campervan.

"I thought you were into equality. Nora Heysen style? And there's no such thing as a man's or woman's job."

"I've changed my mind."

I handed him the waste hose.

Jesse crouched down to take the cap off the waste outlet so he could attach the hose. Suddenly, excrement started gushing out onto the ground. I jumped back, trying to get out of the splash range, but Jesse wasn't so fortunate. As he reached in, trying to close the valve, he was covered in our waste.

It was disgusting. It had poured all over the ground. Jesse's legs and feet had been splashed, and there were speckles of our shit everywhere. He looked up at me wide eyed, wrinkling his nose. I burst out laughing. I felt terrible for laughing at him, but I couldn't help it. I took the hose from him as he did the valves up tight and put the cap back on before rinsing his hands.

"I'm glad you think it's funny."

An evil smile appeared on his face.

"I'm sorry. I don't. But it is."

I burst into laughter again. He got up and started walking towards me.

"Jesse, don't you come near me."

I backed away. His smile became wider.

"Don't you dare," I said, my voice becoming shrill as I took off.

He chased me to the other side of the van. Before I could make it to the door, he grabbed hold of me.

"Jesse. Don't."

I was crying from laughter and panic as he pulled me

towards him. I writhed and squirmed, but it was useless because I was laughing too much. At the last moment, before I touched him and his grossness, he let go.

"You are so mean," I said with tears streaming down my cheeks.

"You're the one who was laughing at me."

I stood there looking at him, trying to compose myself. A big, goofy grin spread across his face that did not disappear when he looked down at his poo-stained clothes. When his eyes met mine, I felt like I was drowning, being pulled in like I was in a rip. I tore my eyes away.

"You'll need to rinse your legs and feet off before you go in to shower. I'll take your clothes to wash them once you strip off."

I stood outside the bathroom, waiting for Jesse to take his clothes off. His naked body was mere feet away from me, and I couldn't stop thinking about it. His tanned, broad shoulders and chest. His solid abs and the way they stretched down his body, adding definition to his tapered waist, ending in that magical V. The trail of fine hair leading down to his big bulge. When the door opened, I could see his naked back in the mirror. I was so distracted looking at his reflection; I didn't notice that he was passing his clothes out until he said my name.

"Uh...yeah...right," I said. I grabbed his clothes, blushing furiously.

When I got back from the laundry, Jesse was standing in the middle of the van with a towel wrapped around his waist. I stood and stared, imagining how easy it would be to undo the towel and watch it fall to the ground. I imagined my lips caressing his broad shoulders before kissing the nape of his neck, slowly, tenderly making my way to his lips. All the while, he would press his nakedness against me, my hand would be trailing down his back, reaching for his...

"Evie?"

"What? Nothing," I said.

I stepped backwards, bumping into the door, nearly falling through it as it opened behind me. I was so embarrassed I stepped out and walked to the other side of the van where he couldn't see me. I pressed my forehead against the van, willing the coldness I felt to envelop me.

Wiping my sweaty palms off on my shorts, I went back in.

"Are you alright?" Jesse asked.

Thankfully, he was dressed, and I could wrangle in my wild thoughts.

"Yes, I'm fine."

I avoided eye contact with him and started to get the ingredients out for dinner. Jesse started chopping vegetables while I browned the mince for our Bolognese. I was having trouble being so close to him. When I looked at him, he'd catch me doing so. My only response was to look away. When his arm touched mine, I felt his warmth. His touch made my skin tingle. I was conflicted. Part of me wanted to stay there to enjoy his warmth. But the other part was telling me to move away, to not tempt fate.

"Are we watching another movie tonight?"

"Sure. How about you choose an animal this time?"

"An animal? What about horses?"

"Geez, that's not easy. OK, let's go with the Man from Snowy River."

I could have chosen the Light Horsemen or Phar Lap, but they would likely have made me cry. That would be a great mixture with all these sex hormones raging through my body.

"Can you finish dinner off while I go hang the washing up, please?" I asked.

"Sure."

It was a good excuse to get out of there, to give myself a stern talking to. But it wasn't doing me any good. I tried to tell myself having sex with Jesse was not a good idea. But my evil side would not agree, arguing that everyone had physical needs. I tried to tell myself I needed to open up more with him; explain what baggage I came with. My wicked side said the only thing I needed to open were my legs. I tried to tell myself I didn't know him well enough yet. But my evil side said I was being ridiculous, seeing it was obvious I was falling in love with him. I couldn't even deny that.

I knew Jesse was nothing like Nick. Nick would never have shown his fear like Jesse had. That would be a sign of weakness and Nick would never show weakness. He would have blamed me. His fear would have shown as anger instead, and I would have had to pay for making him look like an idiot.

It would have been the same when the accident with the waste outlet had happened. Not that it would have happened, because Nick wouldn't have touched it in the first place.

One thing was for certain: Jesse was nothing like Nick, and I needed to stop comparing them.

I headed back to the campervan with no decision made.

Before we started the movie, as we were sitting side by side on the bed, I moved so I was facing Jesse. It was time.

"Jesse, I want to tell you about Nick. I want you to understand why I'm scared to love you."

"OK," he said quietly.

"Things were good at first. Or at least I thought they

were. But that's probably because I had my rose-coloured glasses on. I was young, vulnerable, and he knew exactly how to target me. He knew the right things to say to make me feel I was understood, that I was wanted. He made me believe he was my ticket to being loved unconditionally."

I wanted to look at Jesse, to gauge his reaction. But if I did, I may not have continued, so I looked down at the bed instead.

"Nick always expected compliments. He wanted to know how great he was, how attractive, how good he was at everything. He would bask in those compliments. I didn't notice at first because when you start a relationship, you are always giving compliments anyway. And he gave them too, at first, but that quickly died off. My friends thought he was fabulous, so when he started to change, it made me think I was being too sensitive.

"If I called him out on it, he would get angry with me. He would say how much better he was than me, and I should be happy he stayed with me. I thought it was true; no one could love me like he did. I figured it wasn't worth saying anything, because things were worse when I did. So, I kept my thoughts and feelings to myself.

"He controlled everything. Who I spoke to, what I wore, who I saw, what I said. I was trapped in a nightmare. I did everything I could to keep the peace...for six years...I was trapped, every year worse than the last."

My thoughts were no longer coherent and flowing. I could feel myself changing topic. I didn't know if he was following my thought process. It didn't matter. I just needed to get it out. Share the nightmare with someone.

"I wanted to...I just wanted..." I couldn't bring myself to say how I just wanted to be free. Sometimes I thought of dying for freedom. I shook my head and started again.

"If someone paid attention to me or said something nice about me, he would turn it around to himself, like it was his greatness that made me who I was. Then, when we were in private, he would beat it into me. At first, he would only beat me with his words, but in the end, it became physical. Each time he hit me, it was worse."

Shuddering, I closed my eyes as I remembered the beatings. How he was powerful. And I was weak. I vowed I would never go through that again. That if the only way to protect myself was to stop people from getting too close, then that's what I would do. That's what I had done for two years.

Until Jesse.

"I tried to escape. I tried to leave him more than once. I had no friends left to turn to. I was isolated. I tried taking shelter with my family. But they sided with him. He convinced them I was the crazy one, and the only safe place was with him. So, they would call him to tell him I was there. And just like that, he would come and get me, and the nightmare would start all over again."

I still couldn't look at him, and I wanted to stop, it felt too real, too close, but I had to tell him the last part of the story. I had remained detached from it for two years. Now, as I was preparing to say the words, all the feelings came rushing back. The fear that would constrict my throat. The way I would always flinch at Nick's abrupt movements, scared he was going to strike. How I tried to make myself invisible.

I drew my legs up to my chest, wrapped my arms around them, and clenched my hands together.

"The last time they handed me back, he didn't even wait until we got home before he hit me. He smashed my head into the window of the car, repeatedly, his malice never receding. It was dark. No one could see the blood gushing down my face. No one could hear my screams. I remember the blood staining my eyes. How the streetlights streaming past the windows were tainted in red. I tried to open the door, to escape, but he had locked it.

"When we got home, he dragged me inside by the hair. He threw me to the ground and kicked me. And kicked me. In the ribs. In the back. I was in so much pain I couldn't even scream. I wanted to scream. I wanted someone to come and help me. When the last blow came it connected with my head. The force knocked me out. I woke hours later, curled up on the cold floor. There wasn't a part of me that didn't scream in agony. I had broken ribs, a cracked cheekbone and eye socket. I couldn't move. I couldn't breathe. I wanted to cry, but the pain was too excruciating."

The pain came rushing back to me. I reached up and touched my cheek. When I opened my mouth to talk, I felt the pain I had that day, like someone was stabbing me in the eye. I know now that pain was the movement of my broken bones. My breathing shallowed, responding to my memory of how I had taken in just enough oxygen to survive.

I braced myself. I wasn't there anymore. I was with Jesse, opening my soul. I took a deep breath and the ghost of pain disappeared.

"When Nick left for work the next morning, he didn't even look at my crumpled form on the floor. He walked past me as if I didn't even exist. Like I was a piece of dirt.

"After he left the house, and I knew he wasn't coming back, I called work. I spoke to the only friend I had left in the world. We had hidden our friendship to keep us both safe. To cover our tracks, my friend told our boss I had called in sick. Then he faked a call from his sick mum, and he came to get me.

"He helped me get out. I left everything behind. I knew Nick would hunt me down. If he found me, he would kill me. I moved to Melbourne from Sydney. I didn't know anyone. My friend found me a shelter to live in for a couple of months. I changed my name, scared Nick would find me. My friend helped with that, too. He gave me money to start over. He gave me a new life. If it weren't for him, I'd be dead. I have no doubt about it.

"I had nothing, but I had my life. I was saved."

I didn't look at him until I finished my story. The story of what made me what I am; someone who was too afraid to truly let anyone in. Someone who shared bits of her life, bits of herself with people, but never fully trusting anyone to be able to share it all.

Until now.

And if anyone asked me why I decided to share it with Jesse, the answer would be so complicated I couldn't even begin to explain it. Maybe it was because of the way he trusted me today and depended on me when he was so terrified. Maybe it was because he never pushed me, allowing me to unfold at my own pace, no matter how painstakingly slow it was. Maybe it was because I wanted to be loved, the way I deserved to be loved. And maybe I didn't think that could happen, that Jesse could really love me, unless I opened up to him.

When I looked up at Jesse, I was wide open. He was crying silent tears. Anything he said then could have caused me to wither and die, but he said the strongest words possible.

"I love you, Evie Ordell. I will love and protect you until the day I die."

CHAPTER TWENTY

JESSE

THE NEXT MORNING, before I picked up the phone to call my mother, I thought about Evie's story. It had rocked me to the core. How the fuck could someone treat another human the way Nick had treated her? Everything made sense to me now. The tenseness when I touched her, the fear I saw on her face when something went wrong, how she was scared to fall in love with me. It had taken two years for her to rebuild herself, and the possibility I could take that away from her was frightening.

She said she trusted me, and she must have; otherwise, she wouldn't have shared her story. I never wanted to break her trust. I needed to tell her everything.

But the first thing I had to do was tell my parents enough was enough. After listening to Evie's story last night, I learned how strong and brave she was; I knew I needed to have the same courage. I needed to stand up for myself for once. Evie proved to me that money was not part of the love equation.

"Hi, Mom."

"Jesse, so nice of you to call your mother," she said

coolly.

She had set the tone for the call. This would not go well.

"I've been busy."

"Finding yourself," she said, sarcasm dripping from her voice. "Have you found yourself yet? When are you coming home?"

"I don't know when I'm coming home."

"Your company won't run itself, you know."

"Mom, seriously, what does it matter to you? My company is running fine without me there. April has everything in order."

"So, you have been speaking to April, have you?"

"Yes. She is running my company for me; it stands to reason I would talk to her."

"Running it into the ground."

"No, Mom, she is doing a perfectly fine job. Better than me."

"But no one knows the numbers like you."

"I can see the numbers from where I am, and there is nothing wrong with them."

"When are you coming home?'

"When I'm ready."

"I miss you."

"No, you don't. You just miss easy access to my money."

"Why are you speaking to me like this?"

"Because it's true. You never showed an ounce of love for me unless I was earning you and Dad money. That's the only time you said you were proud of me."

"That's not true. We are proud of you."

"Because I have money. You don't even know what charities I support or what foundations I've set up."

Long pause, probably wondering how much money I

139

was giving away.

"Have you found a girlfriend? Is that why you're speaking like this? Has she turned you against us?"

"I've got to go."

"She only wants you for your money. She doesn't love you."

"I'm going. Don't call April again."

"How will I contact you if I need money?"

"You don't need to contact me. I'm not giving you any more money."

I hung up the phone before she could say another word. I knew before I even called her, all she wanted was money. Even so, it hurt. It hurt to know the only reason your parents were interested in you was that you could give them money. I heard movement behind me. Evie. How much had she heard? Well, the cat would be out of the bag now.

"Jesse?" she asked hesitantly.

I turned to look at her, my jaw clenched. She was walking towards me with concern on her face. I was sure she had many questions. So, it surprised me when the question she asked was, "Are you alright?"

"No."

I needed to call April. I had to prepare her for the wrath that was coming.

"I need to make another call. Then I'll explain everything."

She turned to go back into the van.

"You don't have to go."

She smiled and went inside anyway.

"Hello."

"April, it's Jesse."

"Speaking to you twice in one week. I feel special."

"I've had an argument with Mom. I've told her I'm not

giving her any more money."

I paused, waiting for what I'd said to sink in.

"Shit."

Yep, that was the moment.

"I want you to call our lawyers, make sure it's Walter you speak to. Tell him you want him to organize a protection order. I don't want her anywhere near you."

"OK."

"Then call our security company. I want them to watch my place, you, and the business."

"Don't worry about me. I'll be fine."

"Yes, you will, because I will make sure of it. I don't want her harassing you. I don't care how much it costs."

"OK."

"She can be vindictive. She might start spreading rumors to hurt you. If you want to leave, just tell me. I will give you as much money as you need."

"Jesse, I'm not going anywhere. You're the first person to ever give me a chance. The first person who believed in me."

"OK. But the offer is always there if you decide it's too much. I'll be back in two weeks to sort everything out."

"OK. I love you, Jesse."

"I love you too, April."

I slid my phone into my pocket and walked back into the campervan. I felt my body tense up, scared of what reaction I would get from Evie. What was I going to say? Hey, guess what? I'm a billionaire. I sat down opposite her and ran my hand down my face. Evie looked at me, not saying a word.

I was more scared of telling her than I had been when speaking to my mother.

"The other day, we were talking about my abilities. I

didn't tell you everything. I didn't explain the extent of my abilities or the fact that they've made me a billionaire."

"A billionaire?"

"Yes. My abilities include my memory, but also seeing patterns in numbers and statistics. I use those skills to predict what will happen in the stock market. I own a trading company and have some of the best share traders working with me. We invest for quick money and in long-term shares as well. We take risks, but not stupid risks. All risks need to be justified."

She nodded but didn't say anything.

"I told you how people try to exploit me. But what I didn't tell you is that they are predominantly interested in my money. No one, except a handful of people, like me for me."

"Is that why you didn't tell me? Because you thought I'd only be interested in your money?"

She held my gaze.

"Yes. I am so in love with you, Evie. I wanted to make sure that if the feelings were reciprocated, it was for me, not my money. I was scared. I'm still scared now."

"When were you going to tell me?'

"Yesterday. After we climbed the tree. But then you shared your story, and I didn't feel it was the right time. I decided I'd tell you this morning after I called my mother. That was the first phone call you heard."

"That didn't go very well."

"I didn't expect it to. As soon as she found out about you, it would never go well. She told me you only wanted me for my money, and you didn't love me. But I knew that wasn't right. Well, the money part, at least, because you didn't even know about it."

Evie looked down at the table. I didn't know what that

meant. Was she not making eye contact because she didn't love me?

"My parents have been my worst exploiters from the time I was a toddler. They would enter me in any competition they could. I didn't see any of the prizes I won. They either kept them for themselves or sold them. They never pretended to love me, and only loved what I could give them. They never told me they were proud unless I won something for them.

"When I was twelve, I competed at the National Spelling Bee. It's a huge thing in America with big prize money. I won over ten thousand dollars. But my parents weren't happy. They wanted First Prize. They planned on taking a holiday, and I ruined it for them. I would have rather they'd gone on the holiday so I could go stay with my grandma."

I thought about how much I missed her. She always made me feel good about myself. She made me feel wanted and loved.

"My grandma asked them to let me live with her, but they refused. They thought she would turn me against them. All I ever wanted was acceptance and love. Even when I got older, I gave them what they asked for, hoping one day they would come to realize they loved me. But deep down, I knew it would never happen. When Granma died, I knew I had to get away from them.

"When I met you, my entire world changed. You were different from anyone I'd ever met. You figured out my abilities, but you told no one, and you never tried to exploit them or use me. You treated me like I was no different from anyone else."

I paused and looked at her. Her eyes remained on the table. I couldn't get even an inkling of what she was thinking or feeling. I wanted her to look at me. I wanted her to see my face, to see how much she meant to me.

"You told me your story, and I learned how brave you were. You started over with nothing. If you could be that brave, I reasoned I could be brave, too. I told my mother I wasn't going to give them any more money."

She continued sitting on her hands as she had done throughout my entire explanation. I wanted to reach over and lift her chin so she would look at me. The minutes ticked by.

When she lifted her head, she made eye contact with me and asked, "Who's April?"

"She is one of those handful of people I can trust."

"Do you love her?"

"Yes, as a trusted friend. Just as she loves me. I saved her from a dark place, and a great friendship and understanding grew from that."

"What dark place?"

"When I met her, she was living in her car. She was a terrified young lady who needed a break."

She nodded. Still, her face gave nothing away.

"I can't be angry with you, Jesse. I want to because it would give me a reason to push you away. I know you kept this from me to protect yourself. Just as I kept what happened with Nick away from the world."

I reached over, offering her my hand. She took it.

"If there is anything else you'd like to tell me, now is the time to do it," she said, her eyes searching mine.

"After we get back, I need to go to the states to sort everything out. Once that's done, I want to come back here to be with you."

She nodded again. She wasn't saying much, which made me nervous. Had the progress we'd made been lost?

CHAPTER TWENTY-ONE

EVIE

WHAT JESSE TOLD me was sad. All he'd ever wanted was for someone to love him for him. I did love him. I knew I did the moment I decided to tell him about my past. But for some reason I couldn't fathom, I did not tell him that as he sat across from me desperately seeking affirmation.

If I were to analyse it, it would be because saying it meant showing complete vulnerability. It would give him power. He would know he could destroy me. I knew the thought was unreasonable, but it felt like the last line of defence. I didn't withhold those three words to hurt him. I withheld them to protect myself.

"Let's have breakfast."

We stood next to each other, preparing ingredients for our omelette. This time as our bodies touched, the electricity I felt between us did not frighten me. I didn't move away from his warmth. Instead, I embraced it, moving closer to him so I could feel it. When he looked at me, I didn't look away; I looked back at him and smiled. I thought about how he said he wanted to be with me. That meant not just the eight months left on his visa, but permanently. My heart fluttered.

As we finished cooking, I kissed him on the cheek.

"What's on the agenda for today?' he asked as we ate breakfast.

"The ghost tour is tonight. I don't feel like doing anything touristy today. Why don't we ask at the surf club about a surfboard for you to hire?"

"What about you?"

"I'm happy to sit and read while you surf. Just relax for a change." And watch you, I added to myself.

Walking down the staircase to Ocean Beach, I was amazed at the blue colour of the ocean and the whiteness of the sand. The contrast was glorious. Looking out at the water, I was pleased to see some decent waves for Jesse. Before he headed to the shore, I gave him a kiss and told him to have fun.

He turned away and walked towards the water. After two steps, he dropped his board and turned back to me. He strode to me and took me in his arms. My heart beat fast as his lips connected with mine. He pulled me hard against him and plunged his tongue into my mouth. His confidence and urgency stirred something inside me.

I wrapped my arms around his neck, pulling him closer to me, enjoying the feeling of my hard nipples pushed against his chest. His kiss became deeper, harder. I could feel his erection through his wetsuit.

My heart beat faster. I shuddered as I thought about him kissing me, touching me, being inside me. I thought the tremors in my legs would cause them to give out at any second.

I pulled myself closer to him, pushing my pelvis into his,

wanting to get as close as I could. I felt a deep urge I had not felt in a long time. His kisses slowed as his hand reached into my hair, entangling itself. The kiss slowed further, and we broke apart, breathing roughly. He came back, embracing my lips with his, once, twice, while he held my face.

"Holy shit," I whispered, still holding onto him, not sure if I could stand on my own. If sex with him was as good as his kissing, I thought I might die.

He smiled at me, kissed me lightly on the lips, and made his way to the water with his board. I stretched my arms and legs, trying to expel the lust from every cell. There was no possible way I could concentrate on reading. I sat there with my legs tucked up to my chest, watching him master the waves.

WE WALKED into the Albany Gaol grounds hand in hand. I was feeling the jitters before the tour even started. When the sun sank far enough on the horizon, we entered the gaol. As we passed through the thick stone walls, I felt them press into me. I held Jesse's hand tighter.

Our guide told us the story of the town drunk who revelled every Friday night and ended up in gaol. One night the gaol was full, so they threw him into solitary confinement. The guards on watch heard him scream about someone touching him. They ignored him. In the morning, they found him dead.

Another time, some soldiers had gone into town for a drink without permission. When their commander found them missing, he ordered them caught and thrown into solitary confinement. All twenty-two of them were thrown into a cell normally occupied by one lonely man. The guards reported hearing guttural cries and harsh yelling. Thinking it was mere drunkenness, they ignored it. When they opened the cell door in the morning, the smell that hit them nearly knocked them off their feet. They found two soldiers dead.

Our group was ushered into that same cell. The cold stone walls enclosed us in the dank room. As we waited in the still darkness for the door to be closed, I felt the hair stand up on my arms. An oppressive feeling took over me as the doors closed. We may have been in the cell with sixteen others, but I felt alone. An overpowering smell of sweat, human waste and vomit filled my nose. I tried to breathe through my mouth, but it was no help. Nausea was over-taking me. I held onto Jesse's arm and pressed my face into his shoulder.

The dark overwhelmed me. I held my hand up in front of my face. My eyes couldn't even register the movement. The movement I did register was something brushing up against my leg, stilling, caressing. Suppressing a scream, tears of fear bursting from my eyes, I clutched onto Jesse even tighter. He turned me and wrapped me in his arms as I shook, my skin clammy, my breath coming in gasps.

"Are you OK?" he whispered against my hair.

I couldn't answer. I held him tighter. The touch lingered against my skin. A cold breath swept across my neck. I tensed, stomach clenching as bile rose in my throat. The breath came again, followed by a touch. I could barely breathe. Jesse's arms tightened around me as I shook.

"It's OK, Evie," he whispered. He rubbed my back, and the strange touch left.

As soon as the doors opened, I made my escape. Jesse rested his hand on my back as I bent over, trying to regulate my breathing and keep myself from vomiting. When I mastered my breathing and stood up, still shaky, Jesse turned me towards him and wrapped me in his arms. I felt safe in his arms.

"Are you OK? What happened in there?"

"You couldn't smell it?"

"Smell what?"

"It was putrid. Like human waste and sweat. It was the smell of fear, torment, and death."

"I couldn't smell it."

"And then when it touched me."

I couldn't continue, shuddering at the memory. Jesse's arms tensed around me.

"What touched you?"

"I don't know. It was cold and uncanny. Just lingering and haunting me."

He kissed me on the forehead.

The guide offered me a bottle of water.

"Are you OK, Miss?" he asked, as I took the water from him.

I nodded.

"It is uncommon, but some people have experienced strange things in that cell. Smells mostly."

"It was disgusting. It was like it infiltrated every part of me. But the cold breath against my neck and the touch was worse."

The rest of the group were listening to us, encircling us. Their watchful eyes made me shift away from them, closer to Jesse. The guide stood in front of us, saying, "OK, let's continue the tour."

I hardly heard him as we progressed through the gaol. I heard something about how the local newspaper captured the one and only hanging on film. The local school children came to watch it. Even my muted mind thought it was astounding.

CHAPTER TWENTY-TWO

JESSE

I WOKE up with Evie still wrapped in my arms. Her smell, her touch, the sound of her soft breathing, the peacefulness on her face. It invaded my senses.

I'd never felt so in touch with someone in my whole life. Every day we opened ourselves up a little more, sharing another part of our souls. I couldn't live my life without her now.

Evie stirred in my arms and settled again. I kissed the top of her head and tightened my arm around her. Opening her eyes, she looked up at me and smiled before closing her eyes again. Not wanting to disturb her peace, I relaxed into the pillows and closed my eyes.

Her hand found my face and trailed down my neck to my chest. She moved her body up so her lips could meet my jawline. Her breasts pushed up against my body. They were perfectly rounded. I wanted to caress them and feel their softness in my palm. I became hard. It took all my self-control to keep my hands still. Her lips found mine, and she kissed me tenderly. As her lips drew away from mine, I opened my eyes to see her smiling at me.

I wanted her. I should have dragged her lips back to mine. I should have held her close, taken charge, kissed her, loved her. Instead, I watched her as she moved away.

"I'VE ORGANIZED A SURPRISE FOR YOU," I said as we neared Esperance. "Take the turnoff to Cape Le Grand National Park."

"OK."

We pulled into the Lucky Bay campground.

"See those stand-up paddleboards? That's our spot."

She looked at me with wide eyes.

"Are those paddleboards for us?"

"Yes. I thought it would be something we could enjoy together."

Her beaming face said more to me than words ever could.

"How did you arrange this?"

"Sent some emails to the hire company, begged a little, paid generously."

As we walked onto the fine, gloriously white sand, it squeaked beneath our feet. The turquoise water stretched out before us. Evie was in a bikini top and board shorts. I couldn't keep my eyes off her as she cast off on the board. She was like a goddess. Nice rounded hips led up to her slim waist. Her chest widened, erupting with her beautiful breasts. They were perfectly proportioned and enhanced by her hour-glass figure.

The stand-up paddleboard was longer, wider, and flatter than a surfboard and easier to balance on. It didn't look as strenuous as surfing. But I could still feel my muscles, especially my core, working while I balanced and paddled. The calm, flat water of the bay helped us glide along. I looked at the water beneath us. It was so clear we could see our shadows follow us serenely on the sand below.

"It's beautiful," Evie said.

"Like you."

She blushed.

With no warning, she lost her balance and fell into the water. When her head surfaced, she looked for her paddle, grabbing it before she swam towards her board. She took hold of her board and held onto it until her laughter subsided. Once she gained control of herself, she pushed herself back onto the board. The water glistened on her body. She looked over at me, smiling.

"I lost my concentration. It must have been your hot body distracting me."

This time it was my turn to blush.

"Could you touch the ground there?"

"No."

"Wow. The water is so clear, even at that depth. Let's go out further."

We paddled in silence, letting the tranquility envelop us. There was a hint of salt in the air. It was only us under the powder blue sky. Not another living being was in sight. Soft white clouds sat still in the sky, the breeze so light there was no force to push them along.

The water became darker the farther we paddled out, a deeper shade of turquoise. I looked down at the sand beneath us, and although the water didn't have the same clarity, I could still see the bottom. I turned to shore to see how far we'd come, maybe half a mile. The tide was coming in, which would help with our return journey.

"Shall we head back?" I asked.

"OK."

When we were about two hundred meters from the shore, Evie looked at me.

"Want to race to shore?"

"Sure."

We started off even, but as the shore came closer, I pulled away. When my board hit the sand, I jumped off and turned toward Evie. She wasn't far behind. When she reached the shoreline, I was there to meet her. She leapt off the board and into my waiting arms. I kissed her deeply, totally lost in her.

My hand fit comfortably in the small of her back as I pulled her closer. My hands drifted to her slim waist, her hips, back up to her breasts. The urgency of her kisses deepened. Her hands made their way down my back.

Giggling erupted behind us. Pulling apart, I turned towards the sound. I hadn't realized there was anyone else on the beach. Two young children, with wild curly red hair, around the age of eight, were watching us.

"Hello," I said to them.

They took this as an invitation and came skipping toward us. The boy walked around the boards examining them, while the girl grinned at us.

"Can we have a go, please?" the boy asked, turning his big green eyes on us.

"Where are your parents?" I asked.

"Over there," the girl said, pointing toward two men walking toward us.

"You need to ask them first," I said, and the boy took off running.

"I'm Jasmine. And that's my twin, Julian," Jasmine said, still grinning.

"I'm Jesse, and this is Evie."

"Are you in love? Dad says people kiss a lot when they're in love. Our dads kiss."

"We sure are," I said, smiling at Evie.

"Kissing is gross."

"Not when you're in love," I said.

Julian came running back, his energy stirring the air like a tornado.

"Dad said yes."

"OK. Let's move the boards into the water."

CHAPTER TWENTY-THREE

EVIE

JESSE WAS his usual patient self with the children. He seemed to consume their energy and send it back out to them with unbridled enthusiasm. The kids had a blast, especially when we hopped onto the boards with them and raced.

There was no way I could beat Jesse's muscle power. So Jasmine and I had to come up with some strategies. She was fearless. I had to laugh at some of her ideas, like launching herself at Jesse to knock him off the board so I could race to the end. But it didn't meet the rules, which said both of us needed to be on the board to win.

"How about we get close to them at the start line and I distract him with a kiss, you push him off, and we race? It will take him time to get back up, and we will win."

She nodded eagerly.

I was willing to make the sacrifice.

"How about a good luck kiss?" I said to Jesse as we lined up next to each other.

His face lit up.

"Sure."

We pulled our boards together. As our lips met and parted, I relished in the warmth of his mouth. I hoped Jasmine would make her move soon before I became lost in Jesse's kiss. I felt her stand beside me. Jesse's and my lips wrenched apart as Jasmin pushed Jesse away. As quick as lightning, she lay down on the board in front of me, and I saw Jesse's head break the water as I paddled hard and fast.

"That's cheating," Julian called after us.

Jesse jumped on his board and made a valiant attempt to catch us, but we made it to the finish line first. Jasmine jumped up and hugged me, cheering. Julian crossed his arms and scowled while Jesse smiled and shook his head.

"YOU WERE great with Jasmine and Julian," I said to Jesse.

"I love kids. They have such raw energy and innocence."

"Do you want kids?"

"Yes, I want a family of my own to love. What about you?"

I hadn't thought about that question in a long time. I'd been content in my single life until I met Jesse. I could imagine myself having a happy life with him. Every day I spent with him, I liked him more as a person. His openness. His kindness. His patience. His ability to laugh easily. The way he made me feel safe. Could I imagine having children with someone like that?

"I think so."

The sun was setting, leaving the air feeling cooler, as we

took our dinner down to the beach. We sat close together, so we could share each other's warmth. Or maybe it was because we enjoyed touching each other.

"Evie, look," Jesse said excitedly, pointing.

Some kangaroos had come down onto the beach. They made their way towards us and stopped just within reach. Jesse held out his hand to touch one. I stayed still, not wanting to scare it and ruin Jesse's chance of patting it. The roos at Lucky Bay were known to be friendly; they had become accustomed to people. The roo let Jesse glide his hand along its fur. Jesse's eyes crinkled as a smile beamed across his face. Just as quietly as they came, they left.

Jesse was still smiling when he turned to me. He tilted my face towards his and kissed me, pushing us both down to the sand. His hand found its way under my top and went straight for my braless chest. A deep yearning inside me intensified as I relished in his touch. His lips found their way to the nape of my neck, and I gasped.

His hand drifted down to my butt. He took hold of it and pulled me closer. I felt his hardness against me, and the lust inside me grew. All I wanted to do was touch him, to feel his skin against mine. My hands found their way under his top to his muscled back. I grabbed the hem of his shirt ready to pull it over his head but stopped dead when high-pitched voices sounded nearby, saying something about us kissing again.

"Jesse, stop. The children."

My hands settled, but my heart rate didn't slow. He hadn't even made it to my underwear, but I could feel the wetness there along with the aching for him. His lips stopped, and he rolled over onto his back.

"They're not even our children, and they're affecting our sex life."

We laughed together, holding hands until the last of the light left the beach. My heartbeat slowed. The deep, yearning ache dulled.

JESSE GOT up as the sun rose and sat on the end of the bed to call April. I could hear her clearly through the phone. The business was going well, and April looked forward to him coming back. When he asked April if his mother had contacted her, the furrow between his eyes appeared. He questioned her again as if he didn't believe her answer.

Then came a series of questions about if he loves me, if I love him and if he had told me about the money. After he ended the call by telling her he loved her, he lay back down next to me.

"Is everything OK?"

"April says yes, but the way she said it, her slight hesitation, makes me believe otherwise."

"Why would she lie?"

"She wouldn't want me to worry."

"She asked you a lot of questions."

"She wants to make sure you're good for me. She worries. I've never said I love a girlfriend before."

"Am I good for you?"

"Most definitely."

"You're good for me, too."

"I know something else that would be good right about now," he said. He licked his lips while his eyes roved over my body, then leant over to give me a kiss. I yearned for him to touch me.

Footsteps approached the van.

"Come back here. Let them have some peace," we heard the twins' dad whisper harshly.

"Jesse won't mind. He's nice," Julian said.

"Evie's nice too," Jasmine said, almost indignantly.

"Maybe they want some adult time."

"How much kissing can two people do?" Julian asked as if once must be enough.

"As much as they want. Let them be."

Too late. They were knocking on the door. I stifled my laughter as Jesse opened the door.

"Good morning, kids."

"I'm sorry, Jesse. They took off before we could stop them," the twins' dad said.

"It's OK. We hadn't started kissing yet," he said with a wink.

"Can we go paddling with you again, please?" Jasmine asked.

"What do you think, Evie? Should we take these two rascals out?"

"I don't know, Jesse. I was looking forward to a kiss."

"Gross," the kids said in unison.

"Why don't you meet us down there? We'll get dressed and be there soon."

"OK," they said gleefully.

"Thank you," their dad said.

"How long are you here for?" Jesse asked. "I can arrange a later pick up date for the boards if you'd like."

"Really? We're here for another three days."

"I'll send them an email."

"Thank you so much."

Jesse closed the door as I got off the bed. I wrapped my arms around him and kissed him.

"That was very thoughtful."

He shrugged his shoulders. Not only did I like him more every day, I fell in love with him more every day too.

CHAPTER TWENTY-FOUR

JESSE

AS WE DROVE into Fraser Range, I looked over at Evie in the passenger seat. She was singing along to a melancholy song, and I saw a sadness in her eyes. Reaching over, I gave her leg a squeeze. She took hold of my hand and smiled.

"You know you can be sad if you need to be."

"I'm not sad. It was just a sad song," she said. She raised my hand to her lips and kissed it. "Everything is perfect. How could I possibly be unhappy?"

The road was wide and dusty like most of the Nullarbor Plain we had seen so far. There were more trees than I was expecting since Nullarbor meant flat, treeless plain. As we drove up the driveway into Fraser Range, some of the trees we passed must have been twenty meters high. In the distance, we could see the range rising majestically, as if making an everlasting statement.

We stopped the van and hopped out, looking around for someone to help us. A station dog came bounding over to us. Evie crouched down and greeted it enthusiastically, lavishing it with pats. He bounded between us, enjoying every bit of attention he was getting.

Another dog approached slowly. It stopped a few meters from us, sat and watched us cautiously. Evie crouched down and used a soft voice to call it in. The dog stood up and looked behind him. I thought it was going to turn and walk away. With its tail low, it approached Evie. Evie responded by putting her hand out in an unhurried manner for the dog to smell. His head hung low, trepidation in its eyes. He sniffed her hand and took another step forward, accepting a pat. Avoiding its head, she patted its shoulder. He came in closer. His tail gave a half wag. She continued to pat him as he leant into her accepting full body pats, his tongue lolling.

He came to me, more confident now. As footsteps approached, I stood up. The dog returned to Evie.

"Hi, we'd like a site for the night, please," I said, shaking the man's hand.

He looked at Evie and the dog, rubbing his chin.

"He's not usually fond of strangers," he said, cocking his head. "You must have something special about you, love."

"Just a love of animals."

"Evie is being modest. She has a dog walking business in Melbourne. She has an affinity even with the shyest of dogs."

"Something special, indeed. Only those who have suffered great loss and pain can relate so intimately with other tortured souls." He continued to watch Evie. Shaking his head, as if coming back to himself, he said, "You can park there by the trees. You're welcome to come to the Nullarbar for dinner. We're serving roast beef tonight."

I looked over at Evie. She was no longer patting the dog playfully. Her pats had slowed and were long and steady. The dog was leaning into her, looking up into her eyes. It looked like they were having a wordless conversation, giving each other comfort. I could see the despondency on her face. Her eyes had taken on that distant stare where sometimes sadness would come and envelop her.

"That sounds good," I answered for the both of us.

Evie stood up and gave me a small smile. It didn't reach farther than her lips. She didn't talk or laugh as we made camp and set up our bed for the night. Her movements didn't have their usual vivacity. I looked at her face and saw tears in her eyes.

"Evie, what's wrong?"

The question set the tears rolling, and she sat on the edge of the bed, her shoulders slumped. I sat next to her and placed my hand on her leg. Normally, she would take it and hold it in hers. Instead, she crossed her arms as if hugging herself. I put my arm around her, drawing her to me. I felt her resistance at first; then, the stiffness turned to shaking as she cried.

"I can't do this."

"Do what?"

I was confused.

"This. Us. I'm too broken."

Her whole body screamed of the suffering she was feeling. I had no idea where this had come from. Was it because of what the man had said?

"Evie, you are not broken. Just because you're feeling sad, it doesn't mean you're broken."

"It's not just the sadness. It's the pain and fear that stay with me all the time. It's under the surface, appearing when least expected. It's wondering if I deserve happiness. It's about not wanting to infect you with my bad feelings."

"Evie, look at me."

She did, all the pain and torture were evident on her

face. I wanted to kiss her. I wanted to erase every bit of pain she felt.

"You deserve every bit of happiness this world can give to you. I am here for you every moment of every day. It doesn't matter if you're happy or sad. I am still here for you."

"I don't think I know how to love."

"You show me love every day. You made sure this holiday is about both of us, even though that's not the way it was planned. You helped me through my fear at the fire tree without an ounce of judgement. You compliment me all the time. You thank me all the time. You are interested in me. You listen to me. If that's not love, then I don't know what is."

"What if I'm too scared to ever let you fully in?"

"Love and trust don't come overnight. We have all the time in the world."

She cried until there were no tears left, and I held her long after she'd finished. If I needed to, I would hold her forever to stop her from falling apart.

***

"EVIE, it's time to get up," I said as my alarm went off.

As she stirred in my arms, the first birds greeted the morning. She rolled away from me, stretching.

With sleep taking its time to leave our bodies, we started our walk to the summit on the hilly and winding track. The sound of our steady footsteps mixed with the birds' first-light songs. It wasn't a strenuous walk, and we walked hand in hand until the track thinned out. Kangaroos grazed serenely nearby, not even raising their heads as we passed.

As we reached the summit, the sun was kissing the horizon. The sky lit up like it was on fire. The sun was the red-hot epicenter and its color deepened as it rose into the sky. Evie and I stood there, my arm around her shoulder, hers around my waist. As the golden hues lit her face, I wondered at her beauty. The sadness from the day before was washed away, and renewed life shone back at me.

A chorus of sound enveloped us as the birds worshipped the beginning of another day. The world woke up around us. My heart opened to the enigma that was Evie.

Turning her towards me, I kissed her. She leant her body into mine, and I felt the last bit of tenseness disappear. We stayed there with our arms wrapped around each other until the sun's golden glow had disappeared and the heat of the day embraced us.

Surveying our surroundings, I understood how Fraser Range was referred to as an oasis. Down below us amid red dirt and trees stood the homestead. A mixture of old and new stone buildings with red iron roofs. I wondered at the ingenuity of building in the middle of nowhere. Old rusted cars and trucks sporadically dotted the landscape. Their beauty was held in their age and their ability to withstand the elements of the outback, decade after decade.

WE CONTINUED our 1200-kilometer journey across the Nullarbor Plain. The Nullarbor we saw was neither flat nor treeless. There were low hills, ridges, and trees. Someone had told us the true Nullarbor was a few kilometers from the highway.

As we left Balladonia, we hit the ninety-mile straight, which is Australia's longest straight road, according to the sign. I never knew 146.6 kilometers would feel so long. I would never forget the flies, dust, dead roos every 500 meters or so, and the crows.

"Jesse, look," Evie said, pointing to a dingo walking along the side of the road. "I never thought I would see one in the wild like that."

It approached a carcass, sniffed it, and moved on.

"Are those wedge-tailed eagles?" I asked, pointing toward the magnificent birds feasting on roo carcasses. I studied how thick and sturdy their legs were. Some didn't even bother to fly away from the carcasses they were eating as we drove past. They merely looked at us before continuing to dine.

"There are carcasses everywhere," I said to Evie. "But no live ones."

"They are more active in the evening and early morning when it's cooler. They must have been hit at night."

"Such a waste. But at least the eagles are getting a good feed. The carcasses look very dry."

"As dry as a dead dingo's donger," she said, waiting for my facial expression and laughing on cue.

"Have you been reading the signs?"

"Yeah. There was one warning us about wombats, camels, and roos for the next eighty-eight kilometers. I never thought there'd be wombats out here."

"Where did the camels come from? They're not native."

"I think they were brought over to use as transport while the railroad was being built. Now they roam free and flourish in the desert. I read somewhere that we have the largest population of feral camels in the world. Have you tasted camel?" Evie said.

"No, I can't say that I have," I said, scrunching up my face at the thought of it.

"I've eaten it once. It was very salty. That's the only thing I remember. I can't even describe the taste."

We passed another sign.

"They really don't want you to run out of fuel out here. There's another sign telling us how far to the next fuel stops," I said.

"It must be a pain to rescue drivers all the time."

"We will need fuel at the next stop. Driving into this head wind is sucking us dry."

"OK. I can take over driving after that."

I was thrilled to be taking this journey with her. It wasn't just the fact that we were with each other. It was that we could have conversations about anything and everything; the road, the signs, animals. It was about how we were learning about each other every day. The more I learned, the more I liked.

CHAPTER TWENTY-FIVE

EVIE

WE ROSE with the sun so we could go check out the old telegraph station at Eucla. We drove to the end of the road and then got out of the van. Standing in front of it, we held hands while we surveyed our surroundings. Stretching out in front of us, as far as the eye could see, were mountainous sand dunes made of fine white sand.

Following the signs, we made our way to the old telegraph station. We skirted a sand dune, and out of nowhere, the building rose before us. The broken walls had once encompassed a magnificent building in this sandy, unrelenting environment. They had stood for over one hundred and thirty years in the middle of nowhere, in weather extremes we could only imagine. Although no longer whole, they stood tall like the outer walls of a castle. Sand was driven high onto the walls and into the remnants of the building. It proved how relentless Mother Nature could be.

After exploring, we continued to Eucla jetty. It had fared much worse over the years. Very little of its long structure remained, the wood giving into nature over the decades. But while it was a ruin, it was still a sight to behold. Its piles sat on the vivid white sand, stretching out into turquoise water.

"It's beautiful," I said, glancing at Jesse.

"It's amazing it's still standing, even if half of it is missing."

I bent down to take my shoes off. Leaving Jesse, I went to test the temperature of the water. Cold, but not deadly cold.

"Fancy a swim?"

"If you like," he said, grinning at me.

We stripped down to our underwear and made our way into the water. The cold water licked at our skin. Thank goodness it was summer. There was no way I would venture into the water in winter. Not wanting to prolong the pain, as soon as we were waist deep, I submerged myself. It was like ripping a Band-Aid off; the freeze-to-your-bones feeling lasted a mere moment. Jesse did the same before wading out farther. When I reached him, I wrapped my arms around him.

I had never had anyone make me feel so loved and wanted in my life. The way he held me and comforted me when I felt like I was going to fall apart. His touch reassured me beyond words. As I kept eye contact with him, I tried to find the words to tell him how I felt. I couldn't. There were no words adequate enough.

"Thank you, Jesse," I said before kissing him.

He broke off long enough to ask, "What for?"

"For not giving up on me."

His lips brushed mine.

"I won't ever give up on you."

Light kisses again. His lips were stroking mine gently, promising, enticing.

He pulled us under water, deepening our kiss. I tasted

saltiness just before our mouths formed a seal. Our heads emerged from the water, and our lips didn't waver. Jesse pulled me against him, against his hardness. I gasped as I slid down onto him, only the thin fabric of our underwear separating us. It was big. Miranda would be impressed.

I rubbed myself against him as he grabbed my breast. Sighing, I threw my head back, and his lips found my neck. He moaned my name as my nails dug into his back. The cool sea water embraced my fingers, swirling between them, trying to find purchase between our skin. His hand found its way into my underwear, and my heart rate increased as I felt a deep need for him. I held onto his strong shoulders, feeling the muscles flex as he explored. We were surrounded in the silence of the ocean, but I think at that point, any sound would have been lost to me.

My nub swelled as he rubbed his fingers between the folds. He pushed his fingers inside of me, and my need deepened. I had never felt such a deep need for someone where my stomach clenched, sending pulses of lust through my body. I opened my legs wider, wanting more. His fingers glided in and out. I sighed in pleasure as I felt myself tighten around his fingers. His palm rubbed against me and intensified the feeling, making my breaths come in gasps.

He moaned in response as I gripped his shoulders tighter and pumped into his hand. I felt myself clenching around his fingers as the tremors came. Sighing, I threw my head back as waves of pleasure overtook me. I pushed myself farther onto his hand, feeling the pressure of his fingers inside me. My brazenness surprised me. I had never felt so free to express my desire before.

I gasped at the final release, and his lips found mine again. Salt and sweetness were all I could taste. It was the taste of him. I kissed him hard as he took his hand out of my underwear. I was too scared to let go of him, afraid I would float away from elation. I opened my eyes to find Jesse staring at me. A slow smile spread across his face.

WE MADE our way onto the deck above the Oyster Barn in Ceduna with our oysters and fisherman's basket. The smell made my mouth water.

"Happy anniversary," Jesse said, smiling as he pulled out my chair for me. I wasn't sure what he was referring to. It was seven days since we started our trip. Was that why he was saying *happy anniversary*?

"We met three months ago today."

"Happy anniversary," I said, turning my face up to his for a kiss.

Three months. How much had I changed in those three months? So much that I had the confidence to share my past with Jesse. I hadn't even shared it with my closest friends, but I had learnt to trust him in that short time. He helped me through my insecurities, shared my burdens with me, and washed my doubts away.

Three months also meant our time together was reducing. He said he wanted to return after he went home to sort things out. But would immigration let him come back? I didn't know the rules. And if he could come back, how would he go about making it permanent?

We ate in silence, enjoying the warmth of the sun. Trucks passed us on the highway below, beyond them the beach and calm ocean. It all added to the ambience.

"How's the serenity?" Jesse asked, grinning at me.

"Are you quoting *The Castle* to me?"

Jesse laughed as he popped another oyster into his

mouth. Then he grabbed a crumbed prawn and said, "This is beautiful. What do you call this, darl?"

I rolled my eyes at him, taking a sip of my wine before I answered, "A crumbed prawn."

"What movie are we watching tonight?"

"Seeing we are practically in the desert, let's go with *Priscilla Queen of the Desert*."

"Dare I ask what that's about?"

"A bus called Priscilla, two drag queens and a transgender woman."

"Sounds just like my thing."

"The costumes are to die for. Even won an academy award."

WE HEADED off early for our jaunt to Baird Bay. Jesse had no idea what I had planned. I was so excited; I could hardly contain myself and bounced in my seat. Jesse looked at me, raising his eyebrows.

"Eyes on the road, Rhonda."

"What?"

"It's a commercial about Rhonda and Ketut. Pull over, and I'll show you."

I brought the video up and showed him the series of commercials from AAMI, which were Australian favourites. I loved how he understood our Australian humour. He laughed in all the right places.

"You look so hot today, Rhonda, like a sunrise," he said to me.

"Kiss me, Ketut." I hopped out of my seat and into his lap to kiss him. I would have dragged him into the back of the van if I wasn't worried about being late.

As we drove into Baird Bay, Jesse slowed down so I could give him directions. We followed the access road to the beach.

"It's the place with the flag. Park on the beach."

Jesse did as I asked and looked at me inquisitively. I led him inside the building, pleased I had kept the surprise contained for so long. Jesse's eyes widened as he realised what we were about to do. I grabbed his hand eagerly.

"We're here for the tour, booked under Evie."

"Great. Let's get you into wetsuits," the lady behind the counter said.

Our boat ride to the swimming point was just over fifteen minutes. I sat on my hands, trying to keep them and myself still, and listened attentively to our guide. When the boat stopped, I looked around, waiting to see what would appear. A young sea lion popped its head out of the water. I don't know whose smile was bigger – the sea lion's, Jesse's, or mine.

"Now, remember these little guys love to play and interact with you. It is a two-way street. If you don't do your part, they will get bored and swim away."

"You go first," I said to Jesse.

"I don't want you to miss out."

"Don't worry, once you hop in others are sure to arrive," our guide reassured us.

We put on our snorkels and goggles. Jesse climbed down the ladder into the clear water. I watched as Jesse and the sea lion played a game of chasey. I hopped into the water, and two more sea lions appeared. I didn't know which one to pay more attention to. In the end, the sea lion chose me. It came right up to my face and smiled. I reached out my hand to touch it, and it darted away. I followed it, swimming this way and that, as it did somersaults and tumble turns. The more I encouraged it by doing movements of my own, the more it played.

We frolicked in the water together. The sea lion sped past me. I reached out my hand for a touch, and my fingertips brushed its side. It continued to dive and dance. Excitement and joy soared through my veins. It swam up to me, touching its nose to mine, making me giggle as it swam off.

When I looked up to see where the boat was, I saw it was a couple hundred metres away. I made my way back to it, the buzz not leaving me. When I looked to the side, I noticed two dolphins swimming beside me.

I hopped onto the boat into Jesse's waiting arms. We sat huddled together for warmth, our towels wrapped around us. Jesse talked a hundred miles an hour, telling me all about his sea lion. His eyes were wide and glowing as he spoke. He couldn't thank me enough.

This is what it was like to share unbridled joy with someone you love. His face was alight, and my heart lit up in response. His appreciation was in abundance. My heart sang with his. To think his overflowing elation was something I helped create was unbelievable to me.

Jesse grabbed my face. He kissed me firmly and declared for everyone to hear, "These have been the best seven days of my life. No, the best three months. I love you, Evie."

CHAPTER TWENTY-SIX

JESSE

I AWOKE to the sound of the waves lapping at the shore meters away from the van. Evie was sprawled out, an arm and leg thrown over me. I kissed the top of her head and rested my arm on her back. I lay there listening to her rhythmic breathing, feeling peace and gratitude enter every cell. I closed my eyes, taking in the warmth where her skin touched mine. I breathed in her smell, hints of floral from her shampoo mixed with a touch of salt from the sea.

Evie stirred and pulled herself closer. The rhythm of her breathing changed, telling me she was waking. I let her wake in her own time, enjoying the closeness of her. Her hand moved from where it rested on my chest down to my waist and then back up to my face. I was hard instantly.

As she rolled on top of me my eyes sprung open. She nuzzled my neck. There was no way she could not feel my hardness against her. Her pony tail swept the side of my face; blossoms mixed with the sea. Her lips found my jawline, softly kissing it. A moan escaped my mouth. She pushed herself against me as her lips found mine. I could taste the ocean, salty and delicate.

I rolled her onto her back. My hand found her breast. I wanted her so bad. I lifted her singlet over her head before my lips met hers again, eagerly. She grabbed the hem of my top, pulling it over my head, and our lips met again, fiercely.

Her skin was warm against mine. My hand found her breast, and I rubbed her nipple with my thumb. She gasped as we kissed. Then my mouth was on her breast, taking it into my mouth. I pulled her shorts down, and my hand found her warm wetness. She groaned as she arched her back and opened her legs wider.

She pulled me back towards her mouth as I yanked my boxers down. Desperately, urgently, I was inside her. Moving with her. Her warmth and wetness, the way she moved, drove me faster, deeper.

I needed to slow down. I wanted this moment to last forever. I wanted to enjoy every sensation, etch it into my brain. I lowered my head to hers and kissed her. Slow and hungry. Her warm breath brushed against my cheek. She sighed into my mouth as I moved inside her. Her pleasure, knowing that I was the cause of it, nearly sent me to the brink.

She raised her hips, and I went deeper still. I wanted to fill all of her. I wanted to feel all of her. I drew away from her lips and moved my body away from hers so I could look at every inch of her laid out underneath me, the sun peeking through the curtains stretched across her body. Like she was in the spotlight. Could I ever get enough of her?

"Jesse."

She pulled me back down to her mouth. I couldn't kiss her anymore. I couldn't concentrate on her lips and trying to stop myself from climaxing at the same time. It was one or the other. I drew my lips away and lowered my cheek to hers. Her fast breaths sounded in my ear, feather light and harsh at the same time against my skin.

Her nails dug into my back as she moaned. A low groan escaped me as I felt her tremor. The way she pulsated around me sent me to the brink. The release was like an eruption from a volcano, forceful and beautiful and uncontrollable. My breathing was erratic at first and then slowed like lava when it meets the cold depths of the ocean.

She gasped my name as I collapsed onto her. When I caught my breath, I kissed her long and hard.

I could still feel myself trembling as I rolled off her. She reached for my hand and turned her face to mine.

"Well, that's one way to say good morning," she said.

WE DROVE out of Baird Bay and hit the Eyre Highway. I snuck a glance at Evie. A smile etched on her lips made her look serene.

"Evie?" I asked, looking out the windshield at the road passing beneath us.

"Yeah?"

"Why don't you ever talk about my money?"

"What's there to talk about?"

"I don't know. Nothing really."

"Jesse, you're a billionaire. I get that. And money has defined your life so far, but it doesn't define our relationship."

"Yes, but it is a part of me."

"Sure, but it's not the part that holds me tight as I break into a million pieces. It's not the part that loves me even when I don't believe I deserve love."

I nodded and kissed her cheek. She looked at me and smiled.

"Eyes on the road, Rhonda."

Money was important. Not because of what it could buy me, but because of what it enabled me to do to help people. It was important because it allowed me to employ people, to make their lives better, to make their families' lives better. So, while it had no direct impact on the here and now, it did have an impact on me.

It was strange. In all of my past relationships, I would have rather avoided the money subject. And now that it was being avoided, I felt the need to bring it up and discuss it. Was the money why she hadn't said she loved me? Is it because I kept it from her? She said she understood. Were they just empty words?

CHAPTER TWENTY-SEVEN

EVIE

WE DROVE ALONG IN SILENCE, each lost in our own thoughts. I thought about Jesse's question. He must have wondered how I could dismiss the fact he had money so easily. Money wasn't the foundation of our relationship. It wasn't important to me. But it was important to him. Otherwise, he wouldn't have asked.

Money was a big part of him. It's what had shaped his relationships. And therefore, had shaped him. I should have paid more respect to what he was asking.

"I'm sorry, Jesse. I should have listened to your question better. I should have considered my answer."

He looked at me in surprise. I reached over and took his hand.

"What exactly do you do with a billion dollars?"

"I support a few charities to help homeless people and children. Nearly half of Americans are one pay check away from being homeless. It's a disgrace that one of the richest countries in the world ignores their most vulnerable. I've also set up two foundations. One provides young people with mentoring, as well as financial assistance to help pay their college degrees. It can cost over one hundred thousand dollars for a degree. That's a lot of debt for a young person to start their working life with."

"What's the other one?"

"A literacy foundation."

A literacy foundation. He had remarked back at the cat shelter how literacy was important. The next week, they received a huge donation. My eyes widened as I made the connection.

"Was it you who donated the money for the reading nook at the shelter?" I said as I looked at Jesse.

"Yes. It is a worthwhile cause. Developing a love of reading at a young age improves the ability to learn and stay in school."

Smiling, I gave his hand a squeeze. His generosity and kindness never ceased to amaze me.

"They're good causes to support. Important ones, I think. Did you go to college?'

I always assumed he did. That was the traditional path in the states.

"No. I started share-trading as soon as I turned eighteen. I was a multimillionaire before I was twenty. I had it all set up through my lawyer, who still represents me to this day. By chance, he saw my talent at a competition where I was competing against his daughter. He recognised the predatory nature of my family. He took it upon himself to protect me."

"You are very lucky to have him. You have him and April in that close circle of yours. Both of them have your back."

I thought of the people who were closest to me. There was only one other person who knew my story. I had no doubt he had my back. Now I had Jesse, too. And even though I was too afraid to open up to my friends about Nick, I knew I had them, too.

"What's your friend's name? The one who helped you?" Jesse said.

"Shane."

"Do you still keep in contact with him?"

"We talk once a month. We each have a prepaid phone we turn on one day a month. We have a password we use to make sure it isn't compromised. Once we are sure it is safe, we call. We delete all messages and call logs when we're finished."

"That's cautious."

"He set up all the rules. He is paranoid and says my safety is his first priority. His sister died at the hands of her husband. He blames himself for not being careful enough when he helped her escape.

"If it's a do or die emergency, I would call his normal phone. He is the only person I have contact with from my former life."

"Do you ever think about contacting your parents?'

"I think about them sometimes. But I would never contact them. I don't trust them. The last time they handed me back to Nick, he nearly killed me. I haven't spoken to them since."

"What was your name?'

"Sarah O'Donnell."

I didn't hesitate to tell him my former name. It was the first time I'd said it in years. Saying it out loud felt like a reprieve. I didn't feel a connection to it. I wasn't Sarah anymore. Trapped, broken, thinking death may be the only escape. I was Evie. Free, rebuilding, loved, knowing life is beautiful.

I thought about how much I enjoyed Jesse's company,

not just on our trip, but the months leading up to it. I smiled when I thought about how, when the trip first began, I was worried about sleeping beside him, worried about touching him, about tempting fate. But fate had its own ideas. Now it seemed unnatural to lie beside Jesse and not touch him. If I wasn't touching him, I felt empty. In these last few days, we had become so close. Sharing things with each other, we wouldn't share with others.

The sun was bright, and the sky cloudless. It reflected my heart perfectly.

CHAPTER TWENTY-EIGHT

JESSE

AS WE PULLED up outside the hotel, Evie turned to me with her eyes wide and her mouth agape. A stunned mullet look.

"We're staying here?"

"Yes. Only the best for the best girlfriend ever."

As we hopped out of the van, I handed our bags to the doorman and gave the valet our keys. He looked at us in shorts, t-shirts, and thongs, and the corners of his lips rose. "Have a good stay, sir. Don't worry; I'll look after her," he said, giving our van a pat.

I handed him twenty dollars, impressed with his professionalism. He was polite and didn't judge our van.

Evie approached the doorman, hand out to take her bag.

"We'll take the bags to your room, ma'am."

"Thank you," Evie said, smiling.

The foyer was warm and luxurious. Marble floors led to the reception desk. Sitting areas were sunken, with rich red carpet. Chesterfields in deep brown leather gave off an aura of sophistication. Lamps glowed warmly, and chandeliers adorned the ornate ceiling above us.

While I went to check in, Evie chatted with the porter, who now had our bags. It never ceased to amaze me how she could chat with anyone.

The porter opened the door of our room for us and followed us in. Evie thanked him by name before I gave him a tip. She walked straight to the windows that stretched the length of the room from floor to ceiling. The city stretched out before us, accentuated with the golden glow of the lowering sun. I had asked for the best view possible, and they delivered. She turned to me as I stood beside her. Her smile lit up the room and my heart.

"Jesse, this is amazing."

She turned, looking at the room. The king-size bed with a plush headboard rested against a wall covered in gold wallpaper. The carpet beneath our feet was soft and opulent.

She walked to the sitting area, where a bottle of champagne rested in a bucket of ice. Beside it sat a selection of chocolates from Adelaide's finest, Haigh's.

I poured her a glass of champagne.

"Did you organize this, too?"

"Yes."

She leaned over to give me a kiss.

"Thank you."

"Dinner is booked for seven thirty. You have plenty of time to enjoy a long hot shower or bath."

"A bath?" she said in wonder before heading to the bathroom.

I followed. The bathroom was a splendid marble with golden hues. A double shower stood at one end, and a round bath was in front of the window. Everything screamed luxury, even the two robes hanging up on hooks beside the shower. The lighting around the bath was subdued and warm. Candles were placed on a small side table, along with a glass jar of rose petals that stated, *'bath bliss for two.'*

"Let's have a bath and watch the sunset," she said, leaning over to turn the tap on.

I didn't think I'd be watching much except for her. Thinking about her naked body gave me an instant hard-on. For a moment, I thought about forgoing dinner all together. Just so I could spend all night having copious amounts of sex with her. But missing seeing her in that blue dress would be a damn shame.

I brought in the bucket of champagne, placed it on a spare side table, and lit the candles. The ambience could not have been more romantic. I tested the water, knowing she would like it hot. Hot suited me too because it meant staying in the bath with her for longer. I scattered the rose petals into the water. The aroma reminded me of Evie, and I went hard again.

She walked in, wrapped in a robe. When she reached my side, I turned her towards me. Taking her face in my hands, I kissed her, parting her lips with mine and searching her tongue out. I reached down and untied her robe before slipping it off her shoulders. She pressed herself against my bare chest.

We hopped into the bath together, the warmth inviting me in. As I lay back, my head resting on the ledge, Evie looked over at me and smiled. I felt my heart contract, and then it felt like it burst, and pulses of electricity radiated through my body. Her smile pulled me in, and I never wanted to escape. Ever.

How could I truly be happy with anyone but her? But I wasn't convinced she would be happy with me. Not until she could say those words. The ones she was too afraid to say. Because if she said them, it would mean she was ready to give herself to me completely. I wanted her to say them; for her to leap over that last chasm.

"I love you, Evie, with every ounce of my being."

Her lips met mine, and she kissed me tenderly.

CHAPTER TWENTY-NINE

EVIE

AS I PUT my dress on, I looked over at Jesse, who had been watching me. He crossed the distance between us in two strides. Taking me by the waist, he said, "I love that dress on you."

He found the slit in my dress and ran his hand up my leg. His hand found its way under the hem of my underwear. I leant into him, and he pulled his hand away and took hold of my dress, lifting it over my head.

"I like it off even better."

He pushed me towards the bed and laid me down, pulling my underwear off. My heart beat faster as he took control. Heat pulsated wherever our skin touched. His mouth made its way to mine, kissing me deeply as he caressed my breast. When his lips left mine and found my breast, sucking on one and then the other nipple, I felt a deep yearning for him. My hands reached down, needing to touch him. He took them in his firmly and placed them by my side like he was saying to say wait, this was just for me. I shuddered as desire overtook me.

His lips nuzzled my skin as they made their way lower.

He wasn't even between my legs yet, and I was desperate for him to be there.

His tongue moved slowly between my folds, teasing me —long, languid strokes. I gripped the bed covers. My breathing faltered. He suckled and drove his tongue inside me, spreading my folds apart and finding my nub with his tongue. When he suckled on it, waves of pleasure drove through me. A deep moan escaped as my vagina clenched and unclenched. The pulsating started, and every muscle tightened as waves of pleasure flowed through me. An avalanche was released.

As the tremors subsided, he made his way back up my body until he was inside me. Hard and big. All I felt was him. All I was aware of was his forceful and deep thrusts. His moans heightened my need for him. I gasped as we exploded together. Then he collapsed on top of me, and I held him, waiting for our breathing to subside.

What had just happened? Was this man even real? He wanted to give me pleasure before he satiated his own. The whole concept was foreign to me.

"Maybe we should just get room service," he said.

———————————

"EVIE, wake up. We need to get going," Jesse said, rousing me gently.

My mind was still numb with sleep when I looked at the clock. Four A.M. Jesse kissed me.

"I'll have my shower first. It'll give you a chance to wake up."

I nodded, closing my eyes. As I felt myself drifting, I forced my eyes open again. Rubbing my eyes, I made my way to the shower and joined Jesse under the warm water.

He wrapped his arms around me. We stood there, letting the warm water flow over us, slowly invigorating us.

Wrapping myself in my towel, I asked, "Where are we going?"

"It's a surprise. No need to get dressed up."

We walked out of the front doors holding hands. A black BMW and driver were waiting for us. The streets were still dark as we drove along them. The only light came from the streetlights and our car headlights. The streetlights disappeared as we left the city. I rested my head on Jesse's shoulder while he rested his head against mine.

After an hour of driving, the car slowed and turned off the road onto a gravel driveway. I sat up. I still could not see past the headlight's beams. We stopped at the end of the driveway. The driver got out and made his way to Jesse's door and opened it. Jesse thanked him as we got out. Ahead of us was a group of hot air balloons. My skin prickled as I realised what was happening.

"I can't believe you remembered," I said, taking hold of Jesse's arm. He smiled at me. Another thought struck me. "Jesse, we can't go. You're afraid of heights."

"Evie, don't worry. I'll be OK. I just won't look down."

"Are you sure? I want you to enjoy yourself."

"I'll be fine."

My heart swelled, knowing he would take such a risk for me. I took hold of his hand, entwining my fingers with his. We watched as they unfurled the balloon, stretching it out in front of us. It was attached to the basket and filled with hot air.

I held Jesse's hand firmly as we made our way to the basket. We climbed in, standing close together, wrapping our arms around each other. We watched as the weights were removed. The burner was activated, blocking out all other sound. Gentler than expected, the balloon lifted off the ground.

As we rose higher, I looked at Jesse to make sure he was OK. He smiled. So far, so good. The climb was gentle and gradual. As the burner turned off, the sudden silence was extraordinary. Then we heard birds as they sang their morning song, greeting a new day. Jesse was looking out at the horizon. His knuckles on the hand holding the basket were white, his face calm in comparison.

As we floated effortlessly, we watched the sun rise in a pale pink sky. Wisps of clouds floated here and there. The landscape was like patchwork—symmetrical rows of grapevines broken up by avenues of trees, roads, and farming lanes. Other brightly coloured balloons floated nearby. Our shadows followed lazily on the ground. The scenery took my breath away.

I held Jesse tight as I turned my face up to his to kiss him. The sun warmed my skin and my heart. Right then, at that moment, I knew my heart belonged to Jesse. I pulled away to look in his eyes.

"I love you, Jesse Morgan."

CHAPTER THIRTY

JESSE

"WE'RE WALKING to Mount Lofty from here?" Evie asked as we hopped out of the car.

"We're not here to fuck spiders."

I handed her a bottle of water. She laughed heartily, bouncing on her toes.

"This is going to be great."

"I know how you love bushwalking."

"Thank you," she said, kissing my cheek.

"This is just the very beginning. We'll be walking part of the Heysen Trail."

"Really? As in Hans Heysen?"

"Yes, Hans Heysen."

I smiled at her enthusiasm.

We started our climb up the curved stone stairway that marked the beginning of our trail. With Evie taking the lead, I couldn't complain about the view. The creek gurgled in the distance. We zigzagged up the hill until we reached a dirt path, following the peaceful creek we reached the Cox Creek Tunnel. A concrete path led us straight to the mouth of the tunnel, with the creek flowing beside us. The subdued light and unbroken sound of running water were soothing.

"How do you think they graffitied the other wall?" Evie asked, looking at the wall on the other side of the tunnel. Most of the graffiti was a bunch of scrawled tags, apart from a group of scrabble tiles and some colorful bubble writing that brought the wall to life.

"They must have stood in the creek."

"That's dedication. It would look good if it was artistic rather than just a bunch of tags."

We walked along Old Mount Barker Road, side by side. I marveled at the retaining walls which convicts had built by hand to keep the road level. The road led us to the Fairy Garden.

"Jesse, this is enchanting. Look at these adorable little doors," Evie said. She led me to a tiny door embedded into the trunk of a tree. "They even have tiny windows to let the light in for the resident fairies."

I turned around, taking in all the brightly painted fairy-sized doorways set into the sides of verges and trees. Some were complete with hinges and locks

"Check this one out. They have laundry hanging on a line," I said to Evie.

"So much thought has gone into this. There are chairs outside some doors for the fairies to sit on and watch the world go by. And look, there are fairy boots outside this door."

It was hard not to get caught up in her childlike enthusiasm. I followed her around while she looked at all the details. There were even houses made of balsa that mimicked toadstools.

Sprigg Road was more of a country lane. I marveled at how the vineyards stretched almost to the edge of the road, maximizing all available space. The vineyards were interspersed with orchards, with the same organized rows. Some houses sat in the middle of vineyards. Others could be seen through perfectly landscaped gardens.

We left the road and walked along a dirt track weaving between green shrubbery and tall trees. The track wound uphill, becoming uneven and rocky in places. The late afternoon sun slanted through the canopy, causing patches of light and shadow to play on the ground. When the trees cleared, we could see the bush and Piccadilly Valley with its vineyards and orchards. It was charming.

"Jesse, listen, a kookaburra," Evie said, stopping mid-stride and turning to take hold of my arm.

A rich chortling sound, starting off low and increasing in volume, broke out into laughter. Another bird answered in return, its distinctive laugh reverberating through the bush.

"Wow, that's amazing. It actually sounds like they're laughing."

The final incline to Mt Lofty Summit was steep. My heart pumped fast in my chest, and my breath became labored. When we arrived at the lookout, I reached for Evie's hand. She looked behind us at the restaurant taking pride of place on the summit, her eyes wide, then turned to look at Adelaide sprawled out in front of us. The sun was setting and bathed the hills in soft pink light. I couldn't ask for a setting more perfect. As the sky darkened, the lights turning on below us turned the city into a stunning array akin to fairy lights. The view was magnificent. A light, cool breeze whispered against our skin.

When the sun dipped below the horizon, and the last

rays of light disappeared, I turned to Evie and said, "Let's go inside to eat."

I turned Evie away from the view. She looked at the restaurant and then back at me.

"But the restaurant is closed."

"Not for us, it isn't."

CHAPTER THIRTY-ONE

EVIE

AS JESSE LED ME INSIDE, a waitress met us at the door. She handed me a jumper. My jumper. I looked at Jesse.

"Dave delivered them up here after he dropped us off. I didn't want you to get cold once the sun went down."

Tears pricked at my eyes. I'd never known anyone so thoughtful.

"Thank you," I said, almost in a whisper.

"We have a table set up for you beside the window."

The table was lit with two candles and decorated with fresh bouquets of red, pink, and white roses. The waitress poured each of us a glass of Banrock Station Moscato. Jesse's eyes twinkled as he smiled at me. He reached over for my hand and raised it to his lips as he had done many times on our journey. But this time it felt much more intense as he stared into my eyes. I felt like I was captured. My heart beat erratically.

The spell was broken when the waitress appeared with our entrée.

"Coffin Bay oysters prepared three ways – natural,

Kilpatrick and champagne. Bought fresh from the market today."

A dozen oysters stared up at me as I contemplated where to start.

"This is amazing. Thank you, Jesse."

The oysters melted in my mouth. The clear liquid held in the base of the shell—an indication the oysters were super fresh—spread across my tongue, the rich saltiness awakening my tastebuds from their slumber.

I wanted to get up, sit in his lap, and kiss him but settled for entwining my leg with his. I listened to the music piping through the speakers. It wasn't just any music. It was our favourite songs from our trip—songs we both loved and sang along to. Right then, *Bohemian Rhapsody* was playing.

"Jesse, the music. They're our songs."

He smiled at me.

"This day has been perfect. Thank you."

"You're welcome."

I couldn't resist kissing him anymore. And what did it matter? There was no one else in the restaurant. He moved his chair back so I could sit on his lap. My hands embraced his face, my only thoughts on his tender lips, and how kissing them made my heart race.

I whispered in his ear, "I love you, Jesse."

"Not as much as I love you, Evie."

We sat there, his warm arms around me until our main meal arrived.

"Wagyu beef, a decent size, medium to well done, the way you like it, so we've been told. Served with a creamy, buttery mashed potato to die for, on the side because who wants the juices ruining a perfectly good mash. Served with honeyed carrots and beans," the waitress said, smiling as she placed the plates on the table. "Jesse, you sure know the way to a woman's heart."

"He sure does," I agreed.

"Only yours," he said, giving me one last kiss before I returned to my seat.

The meat was divine, and the mash certainly was to die for. I had no idea how he could possibly top it. And then dessert came. The most decadent chocolate dessert of all time. Cherry ripe, chocolate molten lava cake with rich, dark sauce erupting from its centre, served with rich chocolate ice-cream.

"Oh my God, that's nearly better than sex," I declared as I finished my last mouthful.

"I'm glad you said nearly."

"Do you think it's better than sex?'

"Not even close."

He looked at me, biting his lip.

"I have something else for you."

What could he possibly have that could make this night even more perfect?

He stood up and wiped his hands on his napkin. His lips curved into a small smile that twitched before disappearing. I watched him walk around to my side of the table, shaking his hands. He reached for my hand, his was warm and moist, which was totally unlike him. I took it and stood. I was aware of nothing else but him in that moment. I could feel my heart beating faster. I held my breath. And waited.

"Evie, I love you. You have taught me more about love in the last few months than I have known in my whole life." His voice dropped an octave or two. He reached into his pocket and pulled out a box. I watched, dumbfounded, as he knelt on one knee. "Will you marry me?"

I was utterly speechless. He must have bought the ring

after he dropped me off at the hotel that morning. I wondered where he had disappeared to. I looked down at his piercing blue eyes and nodded vigorously.

"Yes."

He stood up and took me into his arms, kissing me long and fervently while the city lights twinkled outside and the waitress and chef clapped.

DISTANTLY, I heard a phone ring. I felt Jesse untangle himself from me, and he spoke quietly as he answered. The tone of his voice changed as the call went on. I opened my eyes to see him pacing, running his hand through his hair. Distracted, I admired my engagement ring. Gold with a solitary diamond enclosed in prongs of delicate scrolls. I loved it.

My attention was drawn back to Jesse when he said angrily, "I'll be back soon."

As he sat heavily on the bed, I sat next to him and rested my hand on his leg. He rubbed the back of his neck, then took my hand.

"That was Walter. He's been contacted by my mother's lawyer. She's making a claim on my business and money. I need to go back to sort it out."

"I thought Walter had it set up so she couldn't touch it?"

"He has, but he said it would be easier if I were back there to sign all the paperwork."

"OK. Then that's what you have to do," I said, giving his hand a squeeze. I hated seeing him like this. It felt like anytime his mother was mentioned, his mood changed. "I can go with you if you like."

"No. I don't want you anywhere near her. She's poison."

"Is April OK?" I asked, concerned his mother may have done something to her.

"Walter says she is. But I suspect my mother has been harassing her."

I nodded.

"Your visa will allow you to come back, though, won't it?"

"Yes, they'll allow me to stay the remainder of the twelve months."

"Then what?"

"I'll get Walter to work on a permanent visa."

I felt like my heart was being squashed, but I didn't want Jesse to see it. Just the thought of being apart from him made me sad. It felt like a vital part of me was disappearing.

"Why don't you book a flight and I'll take you to the airport?"

"No. I'm not ready to go yet. I'm not ready to leave you."

"Jesse, it's OK. The sooner you go, the sooner you can come back."

He looked at me. The pain on his face reflected that in my heart.

CHAPTER THIRTY-TWO

JESSE

I WALKED to the car waiting to take me to Walter's office, thinking about how empty I felt without Evie by my side. Throughout the flight, I had tried to tell myself it was a good idea Evie hadn't joined me. But as the loneliness had settled in, I found it harder to convince myself.

April and Walter looked at me as I walked into the conference room. I almost laughed when their eyes widened, and their mouths fell open at my appearance. I was still wearing my shorts, singlet, and thongs. My hair was a mess, and the three-day growth on my face wasn't my usual clean-shaven appearance.

"Look at what the cat dragged in," April said.

Walter got up to embrace me.

"Jesse, son, it's great to have you back. How was your trip?"

"Wonderful."

I smiled, thinking about how I couldn't wait to get back to Evie.

"April tells me you've met a girl."

"Evie. I asked her to marry me."

April stood, almost knocking over her chair. "You did what?"

"Calm your farm. I asked her to marry me. She said yes."

"Calm my what?"

"Your farm. It means relax."

She rolled her eyes at me. "Do you know anything about this girl?"

"I know everything. I know one of the first questions she asked after my call with Walter was if you were alright. Someone she doesn't even know, but who I care about deeply."

"Does she know about your money?" Walter asked, his eyebrows drawing together.

"Yes. She doesn't care about it. Her words were, 'it doesn't define our relationship.' And honest to God, it doesn't."

"Still, a prenuptial would be a good idea."

"She won't care."

"That means you are going back to Australia, then? Or is she coming to live here?" April asked.

"I'm going back as soon as this is all over. I need to talk to you and our employees about the business. I'm happy to keep it as it is. But it's not up to me; it's for you all to decide."

"Let's sort out one problem at a time," Walter said. "Starting with your parents."

"What do they want?"

"Everything. Your money. Your assets. The business. They have no right to any of it. All the lawyers at the firm concur."

"What do you suggest we do?"

"I suggest we give them a token amount, so they go

away. Get it over and done with. Make them sign a non-disclosure contract and a no further claim agreement."

"How much?'

"I don't know how much will satisfy them. They're greedy."

"I would rather give them nothing. That money can be better spent on my foundations."

"I know. Let's try two million. I hate giving them that much, they don't deserve any, but it is just a tiny proportion of your fortune."

"OK. Then they can be gone once and for all." I stood up. "April, I'll meet you at the office in two hours. Can you make sure everyone is there, please?"

"Sure."

I hopped into the car and directed the driver to my apartment. I dialed Evie's number, longing to hear her voice.

"Hello," Evie said sleepily. I remembered how she would snuggle closer to me in those waking moments.

"Hi, Evie."

"Jesse, how are you? How was your flight? What's happening?" she asked, sounding instantly awake. "I miss you."

"I miss you, too. The flight was long and boring without you beside me."

I told her about the meeting.

"I think that's very generous. Thank goodness Walter invested the original funds, so they have no real claim."

"Yes, otherwise, this could be completely different. How was your drive back to Melbourne?"

"Not the same without you. I didn't stop anywhere except for toilet breaks and food."

"Are you working today?"

"No. I still have the rest of the week off."

"I'm talking to everyone at the firm later to decide what we're going to do when I leave."

"Do you think that will go OK?"

I looked out the window at the buildings and traffic. This city had been my home for eight years, but I felt disconnected from it. Even though my life was here, my business and April, I did not hold it dear.

"I hope so. It won't be much different from what we've been doing for the last three months. I'd rather them stay working for me. They're the best at what they do. But it's not just for my sake. They earn more with me, which means more stability and opportunities for their family."

"What happens if they say no?"

"I'll wind up the business. I don't need any more money. I do it to keep my brain active, people employed, and to support others."

"Walking dogs will keep your body active but not so much your brain."

"I can think of better ways you can keep my body active."

I went hard just thinking about having sex with her.

"Yes, me too." I heard the smile in her voice.

AFTER HAVING a quick catch-up with Laurens, the door man, I made my way up to my penthouse apartment. It was completely modern, painted in black, white and grey. Beach floorboards helped with the open, airy feeling. I walked into the living area and stood at the floor-to-ceiling windows. A view of the city stretched in front of me. I had bought the apartment for that view alone. This, I would miss.

I turned to the kitchen with its multiple brushed, stainless steel ovens, and the huge fridge. I never used it to its full capacity. I never cooked for a hoard. Usually, it was just myself unless April came over. I hoped she would come over tonight and cook. I wanted to spend as much time as I could with her before I left.

I walked into my bedroom and threw my bag on the bed. Being a corner room, the windows stretched on two sides. Not only did the room overlook the city but also my fifty-foot pool and beautiful sandstone deck.

I needed to have a shower. I could not present myself to my team looking like I'd just come out of the wild. I stepped into the double shower. Turning the water on made me remember showering with Evie. The warm water running over our bodies as we held each other close. Her soft skin against mine. Our lips wet and silky as we kissed.

CHAPTER THIRTY-THREE

EVIE

WHAT WAS HAPPENING WITH JESSE? I hadn't heard from him in nearly twenty-four hours. I tried calling twice, but all I got was a message saying the number was out of range.

I kept myself busy to keep my mind off him, and the sudden loneliness I felt. I buried myself in work, but eventually, the thoughts about him would creep back in.

It wasn't unreasonable to think he could sleep for twenty-four hours. I know I would. The flight, plus the emotional turmoil, plus all the decisions he needed to make, plus the jetlag, all made it reasonable to think he was exhausted.

I went to bed feeling restless. I couldn't sleep. What if he decided he didn't want to come back? But I was being stupid. How could I doubt him just because he hadn't called?

I tried to concentrate on my breathing, the way I would concentrate on Jesse's when we were lying together.

The phone rang, startling me from my sleep.
"Hello."

"Hi, Evie. I'm so sorry I haven't called. The jetlag must have gotten to me. I went to sleep after my meeting yesterday and just woke up."

"That's OK. I figured you were tired."

I don't know why I had been so worried.

A female voice called out in the background.

"Jesse, do you want breakfast or just coffee?"

"Wait a sec, Evie," he said to me, before calling out, "Just coffee please, April. We're late enough already."

April was there with him, and he had just woken up? He and April were obviously very close. Had they ever been more than friends? Would she try to stop him from coming back?

"I'm back. Sorry. We have another meeting in thirty minutes. Lucky April came to get me, or I would have slept straight through."

It was a reasonable explanation, but still, I wondered about her. Did she really want to be just friends? I could never be *just* friends with Jesse. And she asked him a lot of questions during the last phone conversation they'd had. Was it only to make sure I was right for him? Or was she trying to show him I wasn't?

I needed to stop thinking like this.

"How did your meeting go yesterday?"

"Good, I put my proposal to them. They all agreed it was a good solution. I told them to think about it, to go home and talk to their families, and come back with any concerns. That's what we are meeting about now."

"What was the proposal?"

"They would continue working for me. I would monitor everything from Australia. We'll communicate daily, mainly about any acquisitions I'd like to make based on my research. Just so we don't double up. I would leave them to their own devices, as usual. We would have a group Skype meeting every week, and I'd come back every two or three months to have an in-depth meeting with them all."

"Do you think that will work?"

"I think so. They don't really need me. They can run autonomously, and April will manage the day-to-day."

April again, "I've got your coffee for you."

I heard movement in the background. She didn't even ask if he was decent first. There was complete familiarity there. I clenched my teeth.

"Is that Evie on the phone? Say hello to her."

"April says hi. What have you been up to?"

"Been doing bookwork and sorting out the bookings and roster for next week."

"You can add me to the roster permanently soon."

"Have you heard anything from your parents?"

"Not yet."

CHAPTER THIRTY-FOUR

JESSE

DELICATE SMELLS FILLED the air from April's cooking. Mini quiches were cooking in the oven. I licked my lips, thinking of the salty bacon mixed with the egg and cheese. She was busy making a light apple and walnut salad to go with our fish. I loved her cooking.

My phone rang. It was a video call from Evie.

"Hi," I said, my heart skipping a beat as her beautiful face appeared on my screen.

"Hi." Her smile lit up the phone screen and my heart.

"Hi Evie," April called out from the kitchen.

There was a slight pause before Evie called out, in a voice too high, "Hi."

"April's cooking us dinner. I'm going to use and abuse her cooking skills for the remainder of my stay. I'm going to miss them."

"That's a good idea."

It didn't sound like she thought it was a good idea at all.

"Do you want to take a tour?"

"Sure."

I showed her around, ending on the balcony, sharing the view.

"It's amazing,' she said. Her voice was dull, and her smile reflected her tone.

"Evie, what's wrong?"

"Nothing. I've got to go. Enjoy your dinner."

She hung up without even saying goodbye. I stood there staring at the screen, trying to understand her sudden change in behavior.

MY PARENTS INSISTED on a face-to-face meeting. They sat across from Walter and me in his meeting room. My mother in her immaculate, fitted suit. Her hair and makeup were perfectly in place. I wondered how long she had spent at the salon that morning. I don't know who she was trying to impress. It certainly didn't impress me. She could dress as nice as she liked, but I knew the person underneath. My father was more relaxed, in slacks and a shirt.

I had told Walter my mother would try to manipulate me, and that's exactly what she did. The tears had started as soon as she sat down at the table.

"Jesse, why are you doing this? We love you so much."

"You must have a few kangaroos loose in the top paddock if you think I'm going to fall for that crock of shit."

Everyone looked at me. I smiled inwardly, harnessing my inner Evie. I loved her so much and couldn't wait to get back to her. Every day away hurt a little more.

"I think we need to get to the problem at hand," Walter said. "The offer from Jesse was very generous, although unnecessary. He does not owe either of you anything."

"We raised him and honed his talents. We love him, as I'm sure he loves us," my father said.

"You didn't hone anything. The only thing you did was use me for your own benefit. You did not help me earn my money. You did not support me. The only person who helped me was Walter. He is the only one here who deserves that money."

My voice was strong. Unwavering. Evie would be so proud of me. Mom started crying again. I was sure it was for the benefit of her lawyer because the rest of us knew it was a lie.

"We've always loved you. We have supported you in all you have done."

"Let's get something straight. This is my money. I earned it, not you. You can accept my offer or decline it. It makes no difference to me. You can take me to court. You won't win. I can waste all my money fighting you. I don't care about you or the money. I can make another billion. Take the offer. If you do, you agree not to contact my associates or me."

Their lawyer put a hand on my mom's arm, stopping her from speaking. He spoke to them quietly, urgently, trying to make them see reason. Mom shook his hand away.

"We love you, Jesse."

"No, you don't. I know what love is, and it's nothing you spurt."

Mom's face reddened. "Is that what your Australian slut told you?"

I rose from my chair and placed my hands firmly on the table. Rage coursed through my body. I was surprised at the calmness and force in my voice. "Don't ever speak about Evie like that."

Turning to their lawyer, I said, "You have five minutes

to convince them to take the deal before I withdraw it. I will happily see you all in court."

I stormed out of the room.

Five minutes later, Walter came into his office, where I was waiting for him. "Well done, son. Greed won in the end. They've taken the deal."

"Good. I don't want to waste another minute on them. Evie is waiting for me, and I want to go back to her."

"You can leave soon. We just need to sort out the new contracts with your employees."

CHAPTER THIRTY-FIVE

EVIE

I LOOKED AT MY RING, twisting it, thinking about Jesse. His apartment was a true spectacle. Everything about it was absolutely stunning—the style, the furnishings, the view.

And April. When I glimpsed her on our video call, I could see why he would find it hard to leave her. She was tall, with curves in all the right places and luscious blonde hair. She was always with him, at night and in the morning.

I was startled out of my thoughts by my phone beeping. I reached over and looked at the screen. My heartrate picked up when I saw Jesse's name.

Evie, I'm not coming back. I'm staying here, where I belong.

What?

My heart felt like it was being stabbed by a blunt knife, twisting viciously as it ripped my aorta apart.

I love April. I'm staying here with her.

The knife twisted and punctured through my heart wall.

April? Who he reassured me was only a friend? This

was wrong. It didn't sound like the Jesse I knew.

I dialled his number. I wanted to hear him say it to me. He didn't answer.

And then the doubts started creeping in. Not because I didn't trust Jesse, but because of my insecurities. I could easily counter every argument. Maybe the distance between us had forced him to think about our relationship? No, we spoke frequently, and he told me how much he loved and missed me. Maybe he decided it was just a holiday romance he got caught up in? Then why would he continually talk about the future with me? Did he decide his love for me wasn't real? If he thought that, he was putting on a pretty good show each time he called me.

My love for him was real. I missed him with all my heart.

But it made sense. Why would he want to come back to me when he had so much there? His apartment, his business, April.

I'm sorry. I hope you understand.

No. I don't fucking understand.

How do you propose to someone and less than a week later decide you love someone else?

I tried calling again. No answer. Seriously? He wouldn't answer my phone call? How freaking weak was that? Couldn't even talk to me? He could only text?

Goodbye, Evie.

Goodbye? That was it? Goodbye?! The knife was pulled out, and life as I knew it bled out of me. When I left Nick, I felt nothing. This was the opposite of nothing.

Don't contact me again.

I wanted to say, 'Fuck you, Jesse,' but I was crying so hard and my hands shaking so violently I couldn't even manage that.

I curled into a ball, sobs racking my body, and an anguished sound escaped my throat. The tears and snot spread on my pillow and then smeared on my face and into my hair. I don't know how long I cried for. When I stopped, I felt nothing. Not the nothing I felt when I left Nick. This nothing felt like hope was now impossible.

I STAYED IN BED. I couldn't sleep. I couldn't eat. The pain in my chest wouldn't leave. The tears came and went whenever they felt like it. I had no control over them. I dry-retched more times than I could count. I had given myself to Jesse completely. I had told him everything. I'd never thought I would trust someone again, but I had trusted him.

I couldn't bring myself to take his ring off. What was wrong with me? Why would I hold on to something that wasn't there? The happiness was gone. All of it. The happiness I'd built for myself no longer existed. I didn't know how I could possibly rebuild it again.

The doorbell rang. I debated whether to get up. I didn't want to see anyone. It rang again, echoing inside my head. I dragged myself to the door and opened it. Georgia, Miranda, and Jonas came streaming in.

"How was the trip?" Georgia asked excitedly, walking to the living room.

"We can't wait to hear all about it," Miranda said, following her down the long corridor.

"Where's Jesse?" Jonas asked, turning to me when they found the room empty. When he saw me, his face dropped. He moved closer to me, his voice no longer holding its excited tone as he said, "Evie?"

Everyone turned to look at me then. Georgia was

instantly at my side, holding my arm.

"Gone."

"What do you mean, gone?" Georgia asked.

"He went back to the states. I thought he was coming back, but he isn't."

I showed her the phone. She read the messages then passed it to the others.

"What the fuck?" Miranda, the most reserved of us all, uttered.

I dropped onto the couch, playing distractedly with my ring.

"I don't understand. He adored you," Jonas said.

"Well, obviously, he adored someone else more."

"What's that?" Georgia asked, looking at my ring.

"An engagement ring."

"What?" Jonas and Miranda asked in unison.

I told them everything. Everything.

"I don't understand," Miranda said. "We all know he loves you."

"This doesn't sound like him," Georgia said, shaking her head slowly, looking at the messages. "He was always so open and...nice."

"Yeah, well, he did a good job at hiding his true self, I guess."

Jonas was shaking his head. "It's not right. Something feels off, Evie. Even the way he texted."

I didn't say anything. There was nothing to say. I had gone over it, over and over. Trying to think of excuses, to find a reason. He hadn't tried to contact me after he sent the messages. He obviously didn't regret it. He didn't love me, and that's all there was to it.

Georgia's phone rang. She looked at it in surprise. She showed the other two her screen before walking outside.

CHAPTER THIRTY-SIX

JESSE

EVIE WAS STILL NOT ANSWERING my calls. I didn't understand what was going on. Why didn't she want to speak to me? Was she sick? Or sick of me? Did she decide she didn't love me? Was the saying *absence makes the heart grow fonder* a complete lie?

But she did love me. I was sure of it. She shared everything with me. Did she regret that? Did she only say yes to my proposal because she felt she had to? Maybe she was just caught up in the moment. Did she feel pressure from me? Is that why she acted so strange on that phone call the other night? Because she didn't love me? I couldn't stand it anymore. I needed to know she was OK.

"Hello," Georgia answered, nearly eight thousand miles away.

"Georgia, have you seen Evie? Is she alright? I've been—"

"Like you fucking care!"

"What?'

"Fuck off, Jesse. You think you can get people to trust

you and fall in love with you before you rip their fucking heart out?"

I had no idea what she was talking about. I felt ill.

"Georgia, what are you talking about?"

"I've seen the texts, Jesse. The ones where you told her you don't love her. That you're not coming back. That you love April."

"I didn't say that. I would never. I love Evie with all my heart."

The pitch in my voice rose as panic set in.

"They came from your phone."

I stood there in disbelief.

"I lost my phone, but it was found. The only messages on here are from me texting for the last two days, trying to contact Evie."

After my meeting with my parents, I couldn't figure out where my phone was. I was sure I had taken it into the meeting with them. When I arrived home later that evening, Laurens had smiled at me as he handed me the phone. A young man had given it to him. He presumed I had dropped it getting into the car.

Silence. Then her loud footsteps. She said, "Give me your phone." There was a lull in the conversation before she said, "There are no messages on here, except for the ones you sent where you effectively ruined her life," Georgia said harshly

"That can't be. I sent at least twenty. Wait, I'll send you a screenshot."

"She didn't get them. This is what she got." She read the texts out to me. I sat down, shaking. I couldn't stop the tears from coming.

"I didn't send those. You have to believe me, Georgia. I love her now as much as the day I left," I said, my voice choking. "That explains why she hasn't been answering my calls."

"Has Jesse been calling you?"

Evie responded, her voice flat, "No."

I closed my eyes. Hearing her voice, even though it did not hold her normal vibrancy, lifted a weight in my chest.

What did she mean I hadn't been calling her?

"I'll send you a screenshot." I waited for it to say delivered. "Look, I've tried calling as many times as I texted."

"They aren't in her call log."

How? How could this be happening? I received a text back. It was Evie's call log. All it showed was Evie trying to call me twice on the day I supposedly dumped her by text.

It was then I realized I hadn't lost my phone; my mother must have taken it somehow. But how could she have possibly blocked my calls to Evie when I got my phone back? I searched my phone. Maybe she had installed an app or something.

While I looked, Georgia explained everything to the others. I found an unfamiliar app in a folder. I opened it. It was a call blocker, and Evie's number was the only one in it.

"Georgia, listen to me. I didn't send those messages. My mother did. Then she installed a call blocker on my phone. Please explain it to Evie. Please. I need to speak to her."

What sort of mother would do this to her child? Try to rip their happiness away? I had given them enough money to see out their lives. I'd only done it so they would sign that damn agreement and leave me alone. Leave Evie and me alone. It was like she had to have one last shot at me for even thinking I could be free.

But I would be free. Free from their negativity, their hate, their spite. As long as I could be with Evie, my life would be complete.

There was silence. I started to wonder if they were ever going to come back on the phone. There were muffled voices in the background. Miranda and Jonas were there, too. After what felt like an eternity, I heard Georgia's voice. "If you fuck her over, I will personally come over there to kick you so hard in the nuts, you will never have sex again."

"Jesse?" It was Evie; her voice was quiet, shaking. She had me on speaker.

I panicked. I rushed my words, hoping I could say everything I needed to before she hung up on me.

"Evie, I love you with all my heart. I didn't send those messages. I promise you I didn't. I would never love anyone else. I couldn't. Not after loving you.'

There was silence. There were four of them in the room, and not one of them said a word. The silence stretched. My hand was clutching the phone tight enough, it was beginning to ache. I waited, counting the seconds... thirty, thirty-one, thirty-two. I couldn't stand the silence any longer.

"Evie?"

"Jesse, come home."

Home.

To her.

EPILOGUE

EVIE

JESSE and I stood in the doorway of the fully restored Flinders Street Station Ballroom. Our closest friends—including April, Walter, and Shane—were inside waiting for us.

I looked around the beautiful room. The parquetry floor was restored. The green paint on the walls was the same muted tone of the green copper dome outside. The elegant arched window frames were painted a soft white. Chandeliers hung from the pressed metal ceiling.

I looked at Jesse and smiled. He made this happen in time for our wedding.

"Jesse, it's amazing."

I kissed him on the cheek.

"Only the best for my beautiful wife."

We walked into the embraces of our friends and their warm wishes. Happiness flowed through every cell in my body.

Sharp clapping was heard above the conversations. "Attention, everyone, the class is about to start."

I looked at Jesse as it dawned on me; he'd made another

one of my dreams come true—dancing lessons in the ball-room. He never ceased to surprise me.

"You are the most wonderful man I have ever known."

I kissed him, lost in just him: his mouth, his taste, his touch.

"Either get a room or come and dance with us," Lachie called out. Raucous laughter echoed through the room.

"Shall we, Mrs. Morgan?" Jesse asked, offering me his arm.

"Get a room or dance?" I asked, grinning at him.

"Let's dance first. We can practice making those seven babies later."

THANK YOU

Thank you for reading my novel.

My next book *Let Sleeping Dogs Lie* is available for **pre-order** now. Here is a sneak peek.

LET SLEEPING DOGS LIE

Dear Tara,

Congratulations! Your application for the inaugural millionaire scavenger hunt has been accepted. The winning team will be awarded $50 million.

To accept your position, please forward your $10 million entry fee within 24 hours of receiving this email.

The hunt will take place in a secret location. Please arrive at the airport at 9am on 6 April, at which time we will text you further instructions.

Thank you for your interest and good luck.

I stood in the airport terminal reading the email for the hundredth time. There were still two long minutes before the text would arrive. I folded the note and put it in my backpack.

A scavenger hunt would have excited my brother, Zachariah, more than anything. When we were children, we would play this exact game, maybe not for millions of dollars, but for treasure second to none. The Christmas when I was seven, Zac sent me on a wild hunt up and down our street, leaving clue after clue for me. It led me straight back to my bedroom, where there was a large box sitting in the middle of the floor.

I stood there staring at it, wondering what my next clue would be. If I had completed the hunt, Zac would have been there to congratulate me. That was our custom. Peeking over my shoulder, I searched the hallway for him. Nothing. Satisfied that my next clue awaited me in the box, I strode over to it and flipped open the lid.

Quick as a flash, something brown rushed at my face. Stumbling back, I let out a cry. My parents appeared behind me; their voices filled with joy. I didn't hear what they were saying. I couldn't comprehend a word. All I could do was stare at the bundle of fur looking straight back at me.

Zac was grinning from ear to ear, his blond hair ruffled, his face with a sheen of sweat from being in the box.

"Merry Christmas, Tara," he said, his voice high in excitement. I took the puppy in my arms. To this day, Benny was the most amazing gift I'd ever received.

That was the last Christmas with our parents.

By phone beeped, bringing me out of my reverie.

Welcome to the game, Tara. Your ticket is attached. Please board flight 3692 to Sydney. When you arrive, you will be met by a driver who will take you to Hotel Cosmos to meet your partner.

Partner. That meant the prize would be split between the two of us. I thought about what $25 million would mean. I would use it to help vulnerable young Australians avoid Zac's fate. It would allow me to honour the memory of the brother I loved dearly and lost too soon.

Shepherd

I sat in the hotel room, waiting. Sitting would be an exaggeration of the word seeing that every two minutes the stillness wrestled with me and I'd get up to pace.

Tara landed forty minutes ago, her arrival at the hotel imminent. How would I feel seeing her again after five years? More to the point, how would she feel?

One day she was there, ready to take on life with me, celebrating our completion of grad school. The next, she was gone. No explanation. No note. Nothing.

...

KEEP IN TOUCH

To be notified of future releases, and to keep up to date with other news, please join my newsletter.

ABOUT THE AUTHOR

Cynthia is a project officer by day and a writer by night. She enjoys writing about places she visited with her daughter while they travelled around Australia. She says that travel and reading are the best educators. Still, to this day, they both enjoy travelling and reading. A love of animals sees them feature in her books, some have small parts, others larger.

Find her online: http://cynthiaterelst.com/

Sign up for her newsletter here: https://www.subscribepage.com/p9p9yo

ACKNOWLEDGEMENTS

Cover by Charmaine Ross Cover Designs
Edited by Salt & Sage Books
Proofread by Claerie Kavanagh
And thanks to my amazing beta readers

Made in the USA
Middletown, DE
17 July 2023

35314510R00142